MW01094707

Seven

By Hilary Storm & Dylan Horsch

First Edition

Cover Model: Nick Bennett

Photographer: Furiousfotog

Paperback Cover Design: Designs by Dana

Printed in the United States of America

Dedication:

To those stuck in life.

Don't be afraid to walk even when it's raining. Sometimes the most beautiful things come to light right after a storm.

Disclaimer: This entire series is graphic with detailed violence, sex, and language.

If you're offended by books that have explicit content, please proceed with caution.

Note from Hilary

Last year I went through I terrible creative dry spell. I tried so hard to write, but nothing came of it for months. I'm talking nine months of writing absolutely nothing. It was killing me inside.

Then one day when I saw the picture that eventually would grace the cover of Six. I had no idea who the guy was and I had no idea I'd write the characters that were created in Six until I sat down and literally spilled my soul onto those pages. I saved the picture to my screen savers and desk top screens and felt the emotion from that picture as I created Blade. It felt great to write again and my husband made sure I wasn't interrupted until I finished the book. Then when I released Six and hit number one in all categories included overall sales on Amazon… I was shocked out of my mind. I had written that book in ten days, how was it so popular?

Dylan read it one night he was stranded in an airport. He messaged me before he took off for his flight and he simply said… Holy shit… I read the book." I woke up to this message and freaked out. What does he mean he read it? Does this mean he hated it and wants off the cover… Why won't he respond? Lol… well he had taken off on a flight and it would be hours before I would know that he LOVED it.

Time passed… like six months and then I met Dylan. We hit it off instantly and I decided to let him travel with me to signings. When I would talk about Seven and how the story was coming, he would come back with such emotional responses as if he was invested in those characters so much that one day I said… You should just write it with me. We both froze and stared at each other for a second before he finally said… Fuck it. Why not. One thing neither one of us imagined was that he would be damn good at it! Like seriously so good that he blends very well with me and it takes minimal effort to make our words come together as one voice.

I hope you enjoy this collaboration because I feel it was the best way this series could go. He made this series even if it was just through the emotions in that picture. We've had so much fun that the only thing we can tell you is… this won't be our last co-write!

Chapter One

Switch

She's here every fucking night, walking around without a care in the world, laughing like she's not trying to make me lay her down and fuck her right. She tests my strength every damn day and even right this very fucking second she's challenging my willpower to keep my word to Blade.

His words ring through my ears loud and clear. "My fucking sister is off limits. If I see one of you fucking looking at her, I'll cut your fucking eyes out. If any part of your body touches her... I will cut that part of your body off. So think very fucking hard before any of you even brush across her as she walks by. This is an order."

My mouth waters at the thought of those tits against my chest again because that's as far as I've let it get with her. She's determined to get to me tonight and I've seen all of her intentional gestures toward me. The pucker of her lips, the slow movements meant to torture the fuck out of my dick and hell even that fucking short ass skirt she's wearing while her tits are perfectly wrapped in some fucking top that's meant to be ripped straight off her gorgeous body.

That's not to mention the fuck me heels she's wearing again even though I've told her not to. *Fuck.* What I wouldn't do to feel those scrape against my skin a few times as I thrust deep inside her sweet pussy. I can only assume it's as perfect as the rest of her body.

Piper is my poison. I know she's going to ruin me if I actually fuck her, that's why I haven't. The taste of her kiss almost caused me to give in to her, but she has no idea who she's fucking with and just what I'd do to her if given the chance. She needs to avoid me.

The front door to the clubhouse slams open, pulling my attention from Piper. Shadow walks in with the newest round of Prospects and I catch two of them looking at Piper instantly.

"Eyes over here mother fuckers." I stand and yell at them before I point to the door that leads to the club table. We need to have a little fucking meeting to lay down the rules before one of them fucks up and I have to kill someone. It wouldn't be too far-fetched for me to choke someone to death since I'm sexually frustrated all to fuck right now.

I stand at the end of the table and watch the guys file in and take their places. The Prospects all gather at the back of the room and watch me from over Stone's shoulders.

"We need to lay some ground rules. Did you see that pussy out there? It's off fucking limits. Don't fucking touch it, don't so much as even fucking think about her. And I wouldn't think twice about killing anyone who even considers doing a single thing to hurt her, especially one of you new posers. Am I perfectly fucking clear?" I feel the glare from Beast and the rest of the guys at the table. I'm sure they're surprised to hear me talk like this, hell I rarely say anything at all. Tonight I feel like there's a few things that need to be dealt with, so we may as well lay it all on the table.

"Blade is on his damn fuckation so don't text him, call him, go see him, or even think about bothering him. Leave the guy alone and if you have an issue, bring it to me or Beast." Blade is one straight up mother fucker. It didn't surprise any of us when he declared his vacation to be what it truly will be. Him fucking Six every chance he gets.

"Is there any business that we need to go over tonight before I send you all over to see Roxie at Club Turbulence?" Everyone looks at me as I begin pacing back and forth.

"The Ink House is a fuckin mess. I need more hands in there to get that back room ready in time." Shadow runs our tattoo house and is leading our newest project. I already had it in my plans to get more involved over there. Hell, he has all the Prospects to deal with every damn day over there.

"Alright. What else?" No one says a word as I turn to face the room again. My palms are splayed out on the table while I wait for any response.

"Just the usual need for some club ass." Trap speaks up and the mood in the room lightens instantly. "I say we do this business shit another day and go do what we came here to do." I can feel the shift of the guys as he speaks. They need some down time. The constant supply runs have kept everyone busy and I don't see anything slowing down anytime soon. Blade has a plan for the club and won't let up until we reach his idea of success.

"Alright. Get out of here and plan to get down to business tomorrow, same fuckin' time." They all begin to stand except Beast. I already know what's coming from him, so I sit down to take it.

Snipe is the last guy out and he turns to look at Beast glaring at me before he closes the door.

The room is silent for a few seconds before his deep voice comes out sounding more pissed off than normal. "You fucking her?" He looks straight at me and doesn't even surprise me with his direct question.

"Not yet," I reply with complete honesty.

"Blade is going to lose his shit. And you know he doesn't even want his sister near any of us, how the fuck is he going to take seeing you act like this?"

"I know what he said and how he feels. That's why I didn't fuck her the first time she grabbed ahold of my dick. She's a persistent mind fuck and I have to say I'm like a damn Saint because I haven't fucked her mindless already." I sit back further in my chair and watch him try to process the inevitable.

"Can you at least explain to Blade how you're a fuckin pansy ass pussy because she gets to you? I don't want to be near the explosion when he finds out. Knowing him, he'd have you chained in the salvage yard because she's had your dick in her hands." I laugh, but he's probably right. Although things have changed since we all first met Piper. Hell, Blade changed the second Six came into the house.

"I don't think he'll be as surprised as you think. All that shit with Six put Piper in my arms more than once and he was too preoccupied to notice some of the shit she was trying. Besides, I have to be the top choice in this house if one of us were to get that chance. I mean think of how she'd act if I wasn't calming her down every damn day."

He sits back in his chair, mirroring my posture. "You do realize she only does that shit when you're around. I've been here in the house with her when you weren't and I can promise you it's like she morphs into some sex crazed lunatic the second she gets to tease you." A smile comes across his face finally as he watches my own grin. "Fuck. I'm going to have to deal with two of your asses being whipped by the pussy fairy. This club is going to cave in around us if we keep this up."

"Ah, I'm far from whipped. Just thirsty." I sit up as I hear loud music begin to play behind the door in the main room.

"You know she's out there dancing for you or some shit." He stands and slaps my shoulder, giving me a slight smirk before he releases a deep chuckle and shakes his head at me. He's walking toward the door when he speaks again. "Well, just don't do anything I wouldn't do, and talk to Blade before shit gets crazy. I don't want to have to hold him back from cutting your dick off." He opens the door and I can see Piper in the distance cleaning the old bar. She's bent over in that fucking skirt and I can see the curve of her ass cheek before she stands to look over her shoulder at me.

"See you over at Club Turbulence in a few." He begins to walk out as I nod, my eyes never leaving hers while she walks toward me.

I hear the big door close outside before she makes it to the table.

"Thought that was my brother's chair." She looks challenging as she gets closer. I don't respond to her and let her stand between my knees and lean against the table right in front of me. If I wanted to, I could reach between her legs in a second and shut her mouth, but instead I'm listening. "What would he say if he knew you were sitting in his chair looking at me like that? Would he approve?" She runs her fingers down her body slowly, lifting her skirt as she passes. A soft moan leaves her mouth when I swivel just slightly in my chair to pin her between my knees.

"Would he be mad if you fucked me right here at the head of his table? It could be our big secret." She's baiting me, but she doesn't realize she's mixing my temptation with the logic floating around in my head that's been keeping me from falling for her shit. If it weren't for Blade, I would've fucked her every damn day since I met her, so every time she mentions his name it only makes this more complicated.

"Switch. A girl can only take so much rejection. If you keep this up, I'll have to start talking to one of the other guys. I'm sure one of them would fuck me. Shadow seems like he'd be interesting..." She's still talking when I stand up and pull her face closer. My intense stare forces her to stop talking and before I know it, my aggression takes over.

I turn her around quickly and pull her ass against me. My left hand grips her throat while the other one yanks her skirt off. The sound of material ripping only fuels my need.

I push her head down against the table so her ass is bare to me. I should've known she wasn't wearing any fucking underwear. Pressing my fingers firmly against her clit, I lean over and whisper in her ear.

"This pussy is mine. Don't you ever forget that." My grip is tight on her neck as she turns her head to smile at me.

"I guess you'll have to show me. Because Switch, a girl can only do so much with her imagination."

Chapter Two

Switch

Fuck. Her ass feels good in my hands. I grip her ass cheeks as I kick open her legs, spreading them enough for me to see her. She's dripping wet for me. Her pussy is tempting, but tonight there's only one way to get what I want.

I twist my hand into her hair and guide her face down against the table. It's time she gets the message about what happens when you tease me.

Leaning in, I unbuckle my pants and let them fall to the floor. I can feel her body quivering as she waits for me to enter her. I rip my shirt off so she can feel my skin against hers. Leaning in, I whisper in her ear, "Do you think it's funny to fucking tease me?" I run my fingers through her wetness again, shoving two fingers inside. Her moan of appreciation echoes against the table as I firmly move my fingers in and out of her. Knowing how quickly she's reaching a release, I pull my hand away, leaving her empty. She tenses up and I can feel her sexual frustration instantly. She thinks I'm walking away from her again.

"I'll make sure you see exactly what happens when you tease me." I grip my dick and slide it between her ass cheeks. “Feel this. I’m fucking hard for you.” Pressing the tip into her entrance slowly, I thrust deep inside her and freeze all movement just to torture her completely. She deserves the teasing so I push against her, allowing the pressure of my dick to fill her entirely, only making her crave me even more.

“So close, but so fucking far away. This is the shit you’ve been doing to me for weeks. Such a damn tease.” She shifts her hips trying to get me to move, but I don’t.

She pushes up from the table and manages to settle her back against my chest. Before I know what I’m doing, I’m kissing her neck and she’s moving her head to the side to give me better access. It doesn’t take me long to slide my tongue up her neck and to her ear.

Her whimper reminds me of how much I’ve wanted to hear her come undone over and over. I rip her shirt open, letting her perfect tits fall out. She raises her arm and grabs my hair as I snake my hands over her body until I fill my hands with her tits.

“Fuck this. I’ve waited too long to feel you. Piper, I’m fucking done playing games.” I push her down against the table again and thrust in and out of her hard. She grips the edges and lets out a long exhaled moan as I continue to drive my dick into her tightness.

She reaches back and grabs hold of the base of my cock, literally squeezing so tight it almost takes my damn breath away. Instinct makes me grab her hand and pull it tight behind her back thrusting harder while pulling her toward me at the same time. Perfect leverage to do this rough and quick, just like I knew our first time would be.

"Fuckkkk." I can't help but let out an exhale as she draws the only word of appreciation I can comprehend. She's so fucking tight around my hard cock that I can't think straight.

"Fuck yes." Her breathy reply goes straight through me just as she tightens her walls around my cock, causing all logic to leave my head.

Fucking hell. I won't last long at this rate. Hearing her appreciate this ignites a spark in me and I decide it's time to give her what she's been asking for.

I grab her free wrist and slide it into my grip along with the other one. I use it as leverage to slide in deeper and deeper each time.

Feeling her body accept me and contract every time I enter her is almost my undoing. She continues to clamp down on me until I feel her release flowing over my dick. Her body moves through her orgasm and I memorize every sound that escapes her mouth. Her muscles twitch as she comes down from her high and I watch her body fall limp against the table in satisfaction.

"Fuck, Switch." Her words come out in the sexiest tone I ever heard from her as she turns around to look at me, almost falling as she does. "Shit, my hands are numb from hanging on."

"You'll get feeling back soon." I can feel a smirk spread across my face as I watch her lips part.

"We're not done here, Switch; this isn't just some glory fuck before you send me out of the house." She pushes up until we both stand. Her eyes find mine before she leans into a kiss that tells me just how rough she can be. Her bite on my lip is hard enough to push her limits, yet leaves me an impression of what she likes. She's working real hard to be dirty tonight. Now what I'll have to figure out is how much of this is her true self versus what she thinks I want.

She slides her hand all the way to the head of my dick before she slowly falls to her knees in front of me. The force of her shove against my hips is her signal for me to sit back in the chair and who am I to deny that? I sit proudly while my cock stands at full attention waiting for her next move.

"This isn't over. Do you know how long I've craved this part of you? I can't let it end like this." *Fuck if her words don't have me harder than ever.* I feel her tight grip around it before she wraps her lips around the head again and slowly works her way down my shaft. Her effort to take me in completely doesn't go unnoticed, even though she doesn't even come close.

I slide my hand into her hair and push her down onto my cock slowly until she gags. She pulls back before it becomes too much. "Don't even think about playing nice," she says in a sexy voice as she runs her tongue up and down the underside while looking into my eyes. Her blue eyes pierce my mind and I burn this image into memory. *Fuck, she's gorgeous with my cock in her mouth.*

She opens her mouth again just as I respond. "I wasn't fucking planning on it." I grip her hair and force her head further down onto me. I fill her mouth and push against the back of her throat while she gags on me again until I let her back away just slightly.

"Do you remember that shit you spewed earlier about fucking one of my brothers?" She nods as she takes me even deeper while her eyes begin to water. "It's time you take your punishment for that shit. I want you to hold my cock down your throat 'til you earn your next breath." She doesn't look surprised; in fact, she looks hungry for it. *Is my Piper a fuckin' freak? I hope so.*

She seals the deal when she takes me to the back of her throat and waits for my approval to breathe again. *Fuck me.* I should not have this much power over something this sexy. How in the fuck will I ever be able to stay away knowing she's exactly what I thought she'd be like?

She grabs my hips and pulls me into her mouth hard. I hit the back of her throat with every thrust and it's not long before I'm moaning through the pleasure of every blast of cum that squirts into her mouth. She swallows like a perfect dirty whore that just got her mouth fucked and enjoyed every minute of it.

"Fucking hell, where did you come from?" My voice isn't steady like it usually is. She just blew my mind and now I have to figure out a way to forget what I just saw.

Her eyes are watering as she looks up at me.

"You can fuck my mouth like that any time you want, especially if you fuck me like you just did." She stands up and runs her hand through her dark hair. "You'll have to deal with me naked since you just ripped off my clothes." I watch her naked ass walk out of the room as I sit there with my dick in my hand.

It only takes a second to realize the chance of one of the guys coming back is high, so I move quickly to grab my clothes and follow after her.

"Not on your fucking life, Piper. Get some damn clothes on." I sound louder than I mean to, causing her to flinch before she looks back at me.

"Excuse me? People have tried to tell me what to do my whole life, and look where it got them. Switch, don't mistake me for a club whore that you can command by yelling at. The fact that I haven't had sex in over a year before you should tell you I'm not a damn whore." I stop in my tracks as she whips around to walk toward me.

"You're different than most guys. You've put up with my shit for weeks and never once let your temper rule your actions." Her tits perk even more as she gets closer.

"You walking around here naked is not a fucking option. Hate me for it all you want, but I'll tie you to a fucking chair upstairs before I let that shit happen." She lifts her eyebrows before she lets her eyes scan down my body. I see her inhale when her eyes reach my already hard erection.

"You're everything I'm supposed to stay away from, but the one thing I can't keep my mind off of." Her words land in my chest and I know exactly what she means.

Same here. She's forbidden and I know it. The only problem is; I don't give a fuck anymore.

Chapter Three

Piper

I can't believe I'm standing here naked in the middle of the clubhouse. The look on Switch's face would be amusing if I wasn't still turned on. It's been weeks of teasing him and I'm surprised he actually caved tonight. I've pushed so many of his buttons trying to get him to let loose with me, but tonight I found his switch so to speak.

He's a jealous man, even though he has no reason to be. Does he not realize I could've broken every fucking one of those guys long before him? He just happens to be the one I feel a crazy connection with.

Blade has threatened to move me to a private island if I even think about trying anything with these guys, but I don't care what he says. I'm a grown ass woman and I can do what I want.

Speaking of something Blade won't approve of… Switch's dick is just as proud as day standing out between us while we both stand here naked.

"Piper, for fuck's sake, will you put some fucking clothes on?" He moves slowly toward me as if him looking at me like that will make me put on clothes.

"Is it that bad to see me naked?" I can see in his eyes that it's not at all, but I have to give him hell. It wouldn't be us if I didn't.

"Fuck no. It's that damn good. If anyone walked in, I'd have to kill them for seeing you. It's just something you'll have to deal with. I'm fuckin' territorial as hell and you seem to have slid right into that spot with me."

"I make you jealous." A small laugh leaves my chest as I say out loud what I already knew. It's just more fun to make him hear it as well.

"It's not jealousy, call it protective, now either get clothes on or get to my room." His invitation excites me.

"I guess it'll have to be your room. I'll need some clothes from you either way." Just then the sound of footsteps echoes near the door and the door knob begins to rattle. He lunges forward, pushing me against the wall. His body covers mine and he grips my hair into his fist to hold me in place.

"Switch. Damn. You have a damn bedroom here, fucking use it." My brother's deep voice thunders straight to my heart. I don't dare breathe knowing Blade is about to lose his shit.

"What do you want?" Switch yells back at Blade and buries his head even closer to mine and I can feel the heat from every breath that hits my cheek.

"Just checking on my fuckin' club."

"It's goin' great. I've got shit handled. I'll talk to you tomorrow about it all. I'm kind of busy here." Thank god for Switch's large body, because without it Blade would see me and all hell would be breaking loose.

"Have you seen my sister?" We both freeze in horror and I instantly shake my head no to Switch as he looks at me for an answer. We're still less than a few inches apart and I'm completely wrapped up in him.

"Not lately. Check your house." I can hear Blade moving to the door and begin to pray he actually leaves. I need to talk to him about all of this in the morning. Now is not the time, since I'm fucking naked. Me and my brilliant ideas.

Finally, the door opens and closes. His loud footsteps leave and we both exhale.

"Get to my fucking room right now. In fact, I'm not fucking playing anymore, Piper. Don't you dare fucking scream." He warns me before he leans over and throws me over his shoulder. I hold back a squeal when he does and another when he grips my ass.

"God dammit. I fucked up. I want you to get your ass dressed then go the fuck home." I push against his back to lean up to argue and he grips my ass harder.

"Shut your mouth. Not a damn word. It's your mouth that almost got us caught a second ago. If I'm going to go out fighting, I'd like to at least have something covering my damn dick."

He throws me onto his mattress before he pulls on his jeans and starts pacing. "I'm talking to Blade tomorrow. He'll get over it." He stops walking as soon as I start to talk. His death glare burns into me as he processes what I've said.

"No, you're not fucking telling him a damn thing. Let me handle it." He's irritated and I decide to agree with him on this just to relieve some of the tension in the room. "This won't happen again if he truly loses his shit. I won't betray him again. It's fucking bad enough that I fucked you, shit I fucked you at the head of his table. This is the kind of shit he'd kill over." He lights up a cigarette and inhales before I start talking.

"He won't kill you. He won't risk making me hate him." I know I'm right. Blade has to know this is coming. Tori will level him out because she knows exactly how I feel about Switch.

He leans against the wall near the open window and watches me. His words are saying he's never going to let it happen again, but his eyes are saying the opposite.

He's already fucking me in his mind. I can practically feel his touch scrape over my body.

I walk slowly toward him, still completely naked and sensitive from our previous fuck. He inhales again just before I get to him and holds it longer than usual. He turns away from me to exhale and I can't stop myself from running my hands up his back. He's just as solid as he's looked since I met him. He doesn't move as I trace all the ridges of his muscles. I can tell he's trying hard to process how it feels when I touch him like this.

His breathing slows the longer I touch him. My nipples brush against his back and he reaches around to grip my hips, pulling me even closer to him.

"You're not supposed to feel this fucking good." He takes one last inhale of smoke before he leans over to put it out. I want him to slide back into the same position he was in, but he doesn't. He takes a few steps away. "Get some clothes on. You need to get out of here."

His rejection disappoints me, but it's something I'm used to with him. "I'm staying the night. If there's a chance you'll never let this happen again, I'm taking full advantage of tonight." He looks at me over his shoulder and I can tell he's torn up about my response.

"Unless you can tell me you got your fill of me?" He shakes his head in defeat before he answers.

"Fuck no. I haven't even gotten started. I'll need months to get my fuckin' fill of you." He moves toward me and just that quickly the room shifts.

He pushes me against the wall and immediately consumes me. His lips on mine, his hands everywhere, and his dick twitching between us.

He's exactly what I hoped, rough and unapologetic with his actions. It's not something I've ever craved before in the bedroom, but for some reason with him, this is exactly how I knew he'd be.

His hands are rough and demanding and he's not easing into anything. He has a tight hold on my ass before he pushes into me. I'm still wet from earlier, so his intrusion is easier this time.

"I hope you're ready. If this is the last time I fuck you, it's going to take a while." His words sadden me; I knew he wouldn't be easy to get to and I knew he'd be even harder to hang on to. His deep thrust pulls me back to reality before I have time to think about anything. Instant ecstasy rushes me again as he thrusts even deeper into me.

"You're so deep." I'm practically gasping when he rolls his hips even harder, sending a jolt when he hits something deep inside. I look between us and can see he's not even all the way in.

"That's right, baby. You'll remember my cock inside of you forever."

Switch

Something tells me Blade knows I had his sister against the wall; hell, it's not like I've let her out of my sight in weeks. So now I can add lying to my list of betrayals against him. This is something I'll have to face tonight, because there's no way I'm going to stand around and wait for him to come to me.

It's just the man thing to do. If I'm man enough to fuck her in his club, I need to be man enough to tell him where my head is with her.

"I'm staying the night. If there's a chance you'll never let this happen again, I'm taking full advantage of tonight." Piper distracts me from my thoughts like only she can do.

Having her in my bed is exactly what I've wanted and everything I've avoided. "Unless you can tell me you got your fill of me?" She's pushing me to react. Her somber look hits me straight in the chest and I can't stop myself from what happens next.

She's shocked when I push her against the wall roughly and pull her ass into my hands. She's loving how I'm fucking her like it's the last time I'll ever fuck again. I need this, she needs this, but this has to be our closure because this truly has to be the last time I'm ever inside of her. I instantly feel the rush from entering her.

I'm caught up somewhere between emotions I haven't felt before and the sexual lust of being inside of her making me crave her even more. I can feel her thoughts and how much she wants this from me. I hate that I match those feelings, if I'm not even more tied up in her than she is in me.

Piper leans back hard against the wall, thrusting her hips into mine and grinding herself against me. I let myself fully indulge in her and she moans and breathes deep but differently than before. As if she's taking in every movement, every sight, sound, and touch like she's making it last. The way her body moves has me mesmerized as I watch her hips rock up and down while I press myself into her harder. I feel her wetness run over me and drip to the floor. For a second I've let her have all control, *this isn't like me.*

I flatten her back against the wall as I slide deep into her and breathe heavy on her neck. "Be a good girl and cum for me now." Moving inside her is the easy part.

Watching her love every single thing I'm doing makes me want this more and more.

How can I ever walk away from how this woman makes me feel? Why the hell does she have to be just as good as I imagined?

I exhale into her ear and pull her off the wall, walking us to the bed. It's easy to lie her on her back because she's wrapped around me like she's holding on for dear life. We both fall on top of the mattress and deeper into each other as we move up the sheets. A long exhaled moan comes out of her sexy mouth, landing on my chest. "Switch, give me all of you. I want to feel you go at the same time." Fuck if those words don't turn me on more than anything she's ever done.

She arches her back and forces herself even further down my hard cock while her hands grip the sheets and she bites her lip. "Fucking come inside me Switch, please let me feel you this way." I slide my hand under the small of her back to keep her elevated, allowing me to fully penetrate her as I roll my hips into her, deeper and harder with each thrust.

Her eyes roll back as I feel her tighten her legs around me, making me stay inside her. She pulls at my hair and drives her nails into my back, sending sensations through my entire body. She's about to orgasm. I can feel her. I feel every pulse of her as she finally climaxes, sending me into my own as both our bodies tighten around each other. I move slowly inside her, allowing every single jolt to flow through her.

I roll to the side of the bed and light up, my mind racing from what the fuck just happened. I ask myself over and over why I would go there with her, dreading the fact that I know I just fucked up royally. I can feel her eyes on me, tracing the ink on my shoulder, taking in every reaction, trying to get a read on what I'm going to say next. Taking a long drag, I look over my shoulder and catch her eyes with mine; she follows my eyes and begins to look straight into me. She has a way of doing this to me and I always avoid this kind of closeness with her for a reason.

I don't know if I can handle this. I have to get out of here. I have to clear my head. "Get dressed, you're leaving and so am I." She tries to speak, but I don't let her, instead I pull her in for a quick goodbye kiss then drop my cigarette to the floor and stomp it out before walking out of the room. *I can't do this, I'm not ready to deal with the shit that will drop if I continue to fuck with her.*

Chapter Four

Switch

The sound of my engine roars as I crank my bike over. It's almost euphoric and calming compared to everything else going on in the world. Why can't life be as easy as this, one down and the rest up. How the fuck am I going to tell Blade I'm fucking his sister? We've not only been best friends for years, we're brothers. I fucking hate this, fuck if I could just use my goddamn head sometimes, I wouldn't get myself into situations I can't get out of.

I spend so much time in my head it makes the trip to the Ink House seem like it's only seconds, even though I rode for miles intentionally out of the way to get some clarity.

I don't know how Blade will react to all of this. The only thing that will calm me down and settle my fucked up head is getting some ink done. I've been saving a spot on my right hand for a sacred heart. I try not to think about everything while Shadow knocks it out, I'm just getting it done. It's really hard not to think about her though. The fact of the matter is I care about Piper a lot, but my club comes first for me. If Blade can't cope with me being with his sister, then I won't be.

It takes Shadow a few hours to make it look perfect and I appreciate the banter in the shop. The Prospects are all in there working and it was good for me to see where we need to work on things over here. We have huge potential with this place and we're not taking advantage of it all right now. Blade and I have plans to move forward on the expansion of this in the next year or so, we just need to finish some of the projects that are currently taking up so much of our attention.

I leave the Ink House and know exactly what I have to do. I need to see Blade and just be just be straight with him. If I tell him what happened maybe he won't fucking kill me, then again he may just end me because I tell him.

I take the same long path back to Club Turbulence since it sits right next to the clubhouse. The door feels heavy as I press hard for it to open and enter the bar. Blade is sitting at a table in the back talking to Beast. Roxy is at the bar running numbers when they all look up and give me the look as if they already know what I'm going to say. "Alright Blade, well that was basically all I needed to talk about. I'm gonna head out and go run by the clubhouse for a bit and make sure the truck is running good for later." Beast looks serious as fuck and has to know why I'm here. I don't blame him for wanting to get out of here before I start this conversation. If the roles were reversed and I had warned him as many times as he's warned me, I'd leave him solo for this part too.

I can't help but wonder what the fuck they were talking about when I walked in though. Beast leaves and Roxy walks outside with him. I watch her pull a cigarette from the pack she's got stuffed in her bra as she leaves out the front door.

"Switch, take a seat; we need to talk some shit out." Fuck, he's going to shoot me right here at this fucking table and drag my dead body out just to make an example out of me. "How's the club been? Profits seem good across the board, looks like you're running shit so well you don't even need me here." He laughs but his eyes pierce right into me, mother fucker is the devil incarnate and never blinks. He already knows something is wrong, so I may as well come clean and end all of my own torture.

Fuck it, I'll just tell him before he calls me out. "Blade. I'm fucking…" He cuts me off before I have a chance to go on.

"Switch, I'm not a fucking idiot. I already know." I don't know if his words should relax me or not, but they don't.

"Did she tell you?"

"No, I'm just not blind to what the fuck you're up to. Maybe it's a good thing Six has me chilled the fuck out. Call it luck for you, but she convinced me not to take your fucking head off. She's been spouting shit about you making my sister happy and some bullshit about she's a grown woman and I can't make every decision for her." *Who the fuck is this guy?* Is Blade just testing me to see if I give in or does Six really have this much power over him?

"But if you fuck my sister in the damn clubhouse for all the guys to see again, I'll cut your goddamn dick off myself. She's not a club whore for everyone to have access to." He adjusts in his seat, never taking his eyes off of me. *There's the Blade I know.* His stare sends guilt through me as I think about taking her at the head of the table.

I nod my head slowly. I won't give any excuses for what happened. "Piper isn't like that for me." I pause because I almost go into more detail about how I feel about her. The last thing he wants to hear, is that. *Fuck, she makes me damn crazy.*

"I know how she can be. She's a persistent pain in the ass. And I've seen how she is with you. Just don't fucking rip her heart out because Six won't be able to save your ass if that happens. Brother or not, I'd rip yours out with my bare hands for payback." I know he's serious. He was very clear about no one touching his sister, yet I sit here after fucking her over and over. I don't deserve his forgiveness, but I'll take it.

"So now that we're clear on Piper, here's the next order of business. This one is just you and me, Switch. No one else in the club needs to know about what we're about to do. Breathe a word of it and it'll be your last breath."

I cut Blade off before he can even finish. "You have my word; I have a feeling I know what you're about to ask." I've been waiting on his call for this.

He looks at me for a few seconds before he responds. "Then you know what I'm about to ask you to do means we're gonna have to get our hands fuckin' filthy." I feel my blood rush instantly; there's only one reason Blade would ask me to keep shit from Beast.

"Where is he, and how many mother fuckers are we gonna have to kill to get to him?" Our eyes lock in a stare just before he grins like a hungry fucker about to eat pussy for the first time in years.

"This is why I knew you're the one for this. You like to go in and fuck shit up and that's just what I need here." We both laugh until the sound of the door stops us both. I look over to see Piper pissed off, storming toward us with Six right behind her.

Piper

"What in the fuck do you think you're doing?" Anger flows through me as I see Blade staring at Switch with that horrible look in his eyes. I know my brother and he can be a protective ass. He needs to learn his place in this or know that he'll have to deal with losing me again.

He stands before I can get to them, only making me angrier by standing in my way like a damn brick wall. "Handling…" I cut Blade off before he has a chance to finish. I know he's threatening Switch and I'm not going to tolerate his desire to run my life.

"The fuck you are. I see you making that asshole face and I fucking know you! Did you really think Tori wasn't going to tell me you know? Don't answer that, based on your stupid ass look and the glance you just shot at her, I'm thinking you didn't. She was my friend first you know, dumbass." Blade's smile irritates me further and before I have a chance to shove his chest, Switch steps in front of Blade and grips my shoulders, keeping me in place.

"Chill the fuck out, Piper. We've already talked about us and it's all good." My heart races while I try to see Blade's face. I need to know if he's really going to let me be with Switch or if he's fucking around just to torture us later.

"Switch, move your ass. I need to talk to my brother." Switch lifts his eyebrows at me with that look he loves to give me when he's going to try to force me out of something I want to do.

"Woman. I'm going to tame that ass of yours now that you're mine. Calm your shit." Switch's voice is deeper than normal and startles me. He did not just talk to me like I'm a piece of ass that he can control.

"Excuse me. I never said you could *have* me, whatever the hell that means." I move in closer, until he can feel me against him. His breath hits my face, moving some of my fallen hair from against my cheek. My eyes meet his, but my expression doesn't match the smile on his face. He doesn't get to distract me with the damn powers he has over me when he looks at me like that. He needs to understand how this will be. "Don't look at me like that when I'm yelling at you. One day you'll see that it's nothing to fucking smile about. And besides that… I'd like to see you try to *tame* me." His grip on my arms tightens and causes even more anger to flow through me. I can tell he wants to say so much to me, but the fact that my brother is behind him is probably silencing him.

"I already told him I was giving him a chance with your ass and we were talking about something else before you two burst in like you own my damn club." Blade's voice pulls my focus from Switch's threatening glare. "Calm your shit, little sister." He stops talking when Tori runs her hands down his arms. He pulls her in close before he says anything further.

"You two need to check in before you bust in here anyway. What do I have to do to make you understand that you have to have protection when you go places? I can't deal with any shit going down with either of you, so start fucking listening."

"Oh, please. We are safer here than anywhere else in the world. These guys wouldn't dare let anything happen to us." I've watched them all go to battle for Tori and I've seen them all make sure I was protected time and time again. Their brotherhood runs thick and by default that means Tori and I are very well protected.

"That's why I want one of them with you at all times. Piper, you're gonna have to meet me halfway here. I didn't even want you involved with the club in the first place, but I see that's a hopeless battle that I'll never win. At least give me some satisfaction knowing you'll be smart about using the security that's there for you." He looks over Tori's head as he speaks to me. His eyes are wild and I can't quite place the crazy that he's thinking. I need to talk to him by myself to see where his head really is with Switch.

"Blade, I need to talk to you in private." I instantly feel a slight squeeze in Switch's grip on my forearm. He doesn't want me talking to Blade about him and I get that, but I need to know my brother is good with this. The last thing I'll tolerate is something happening between the two men standing in front of me. It'll be a terrible thing to deal with and I'm not ready to think about what that would do to Tori and I.

I pull my wrists from Switch's grip with haste and send him a look to back off. He only antagonizes me further by reaching for me again. "What the fuck, Switch. That shit might turn me on in the bedroom, but out here it's pissing me off." I rip my arm from his grip once again.

"If you'd just stop for a damn minute, I just wanted to tell you something for fuck's sake." He barely finishes before Blade's voice is louder than his.

"Do not talk about your fucking sex life in front of me. To me you're still my damn little sister and I see fucking red when I think about that shit."

I'm walking toward Blade before he finishes. He stops talking when I get close to him.

“Tell me you’re not playing games with Switch. Evan, I really like this guy and I’ll never forgive you if you pull some big brother bullshit on him. He’s proven himself more than enough times to deserve me and you fucking know it.”

“I know he has.”

“So why are you giving him hell about us, then?” I watch his face to see his reaction in hopes of getting a feeling of where he’s at still. Why is he so damn hard to read?

“I told you I’m not. Shit, Piper, give me some fucking credit.”

“Don’t play innocent with me. We both know you’d kill someone over touching me, so I’m just wanting to make sure you leave his ass alone. Are we fucking clear?” His laughter echoes through the room before he responds.

“Shit, you sound just like me. Are you sure you’re not trying to take over my club?” He wraps his arms around me in an attempt to make me feel better and for a brief moment I do.

“Alright Six, I’m ready to take you on that tour of the back room again. This time, I’m fucking that ass of yours.” I hit his chest before he has a chance to continue.

"I don't want to hear about you either. Don't talk like that around me, it's one thing to hear Tori telling me stories, I don't need you filling in the gaps."

"Switch, I'll still need you tonight. I'll text when I'm ready." The two of them leave the room and as always, the chemistry is explosive. I only hope to have a relationship like they do one day.

Chapter Five

Switch

Finally, I have her to myself and don't have to fucking hold back my touch or hide it in fear of being seen. "Come here." I call her over to me and watch her sassy ass walk slowly over to me. She's the queen of tease and I'm going to enjoy every second of teasing her back.

"I just can't tell if he's sincere or not."

"Quit. I told you this is all good. It's finally time that we get to do everything we've been holding back." My kiss stops her before she has a chance to talk only to be interrupted by the sound of Blade's yell.

"Time to move now, Switch. Piper, go to the clubhouse with Six and wait until we get back. Don't fucking leave for any reason until we get back."

"I promise everything is going to work out. We can talk more about it all tonight when I get back." She leans up to kiss me again before I move to follow Blade out the door. I can feel his anger boiling and wish I knew exactly what I'm about to walk into. Although it really doesn't matter what I'm in for, because he knows I'm in.

I throw my leg over the seat just as Blade fires up his bike, revving it even louder when I lean over to ask details. He's raging right now and I know there's not anything I can do, not that I want to calm him down. This fucker deserves to meet Blade just like he is.

"That fucker is on the move again. We're taking them all out, but I want him talking first. Keep on my ass or I'm going in solo." He takes off like a bat out of hell and I follow him without hesitation.

We fly down the road, south bound, not stopping for any reason. Topping a hill, I see three taillights moving quickly around the next curve. Blade speeds up and my adrenaline begins to flow even faster. Everything moves fast and we catch them quickly. Blade pulls out his revolver and fires a single round, hitting the back tire of the front bike before I watch the sparks light up the road as it falls, causing the other two bikes to slide out of control. We pass the wreckage and quickly turn around, coming to a stop with our lights shining on most of the damage. Three bikes and two men are in sight.

"You find the one that's missing. I'll take this one and the fucking traitor." I hear a single gunshot when I step onto the edge of the ditch and turn to see that Blade just shot the first guy.

Before I look back, I feel a fucker on my back with his hands around my neck. We fall to the ground and fight for control, causing me to drop my gun on the trip down the ditch. His grip on my neck loosens on the fall and I land on my back with him falling on top of me. His blood drips on my face before I flip him over and wrap my hands around his neck, squeezing the life from his worthless body. He fights me and breaks the grip of my right hand before I manage to silence him forever.

He pisses me off, so I squeeze tighter with my left hand and slam his head into the hardened ground until his eyes roll back and he loses consciousness.

I stand and reach for my gun, sending a bullet between his eyes before I catch Blade wiping the blood from his chin. Blade has him tied to the guardrail and apparently he got one in on him in the process.

"Switch, get the fuck over here." Blade's angry scream pulls me quickly back to the road and I walk directly up to the mess of what looks exactly like the last person I'd ever thought I'd see again, even though I knew Blade was searching for his ass.

"Look who we have here. Mother fucking Clutch. How you been, you fucking traitor?" Before Clutch can even respond, Blades fist connects across the left side of his face, sending a loud crack through the air. Blood drips from the corner of Clutch's mouth and the look on his face just shows he knows he's about to die.

"The last time we saw your bitch ass was on that run across the border; where the fuck were you Clutch, huh? Does the fucking deserter have a response or are you gonna snitch and run again?" This time Blade's boot connects to his stomach as he coughs, spitting blood across Blade's jeans.

"You gonna spit blood at me like a bitch?" I feel Blade's anger growing more by the moment; the darkest side of his personality is making its full appearance very quickly. Blade reaches for his clip blade as Clutch exhales a loud, "Stop."

Blade responds before the single word is even out of his mouth. "And why the fuck would I show a traitor like you the least bit of mercy?" He's a dead man. I can see it in Blade's eyes. There is zero mercy there.

"Because if you're going to kill me anyways you might as well know the truth." Blade freezes. I decide to move in and see if I can get some information before shit goes further south. It's obvious Blade can't even hear him over the rage he's feeling.

"The truth? We know the truth. You snitched and ran. The question is how can you do that to your brothers? We brought you in, gave you a family, brotherhood, made sure you were taken care of and you turned us in like common street thugs."

Before I can finish talking, Clutch interjects, no doubt hoping to save his own life at this point. “It was someone on the inside, someone that knows the club.” He exhales and laughs cynically before he shakes his head and continues. “The only reason you got off was because I went back and destroyed the evidence for them to throw out the case. Isn’t that fuckin’ ironic.”

Blade chimes in before he could spew any more excuses. “Sounds like bullshit to save your neck.”

“I’m serious, Blade, why would I lie now?” It’s hard for me to tell if he’s telling the truth. A desperate man will say anything to save his own life when it comes to facing Blade. I’ve seen it many times.

“Maybe we should hear him out, Blade.” I want to hear what he has to say. If he has information that it was someone on the inside, I’d like to know who the fuck’s ass to get all over and have surveillance attached to.

“I’ll die with my information. The club will become toxic as you try to figure out who it is. Enjoy mother fuckers.” Clutch seals his fate. *Mother fucker.*

“Fuck this traitor. Rip his shirt sleeve off, I’m taking our patch back. This fucker doesn’t deserve to wear my patch. The fact that he’s still breathing makes me fucking sick.” There’s no getting through to Blade now, he pulls out his pack of cigarettes and pulls the lucky from the center.

"I'm not letting this fucker bleed out. Clutch, you hear me? This is gonna get bad before it gets worse. You need to start talking right the fuck now." I try to get a few words in before Blade inevitably nails my ass for defying him. I know it's coming.

Blade takes a drag from his cigarette and exhales smoke as he holds the flame to his knife, heating it to a bright red. "Rip that fucking sleeve off, Switch. Don't make me tell you again. Because I won't and I'll do it myself." I don't move. I can feel Clutch has more to say and will talk. This isn't the way to go about this, but Blade has shut everyone out, he's on a hunt for blood.

"Get the fuck out of my way, Switch. If you're such a pussy that you can't rip a fucking sleeve off when I tell you to then I won't bring your ass next time." Blade shoulder checks me as he walks by and all that follows are loud screams and the smell or cauterized skin. I watch as Clutch agonizes over the pain of Blade removing ink and skin from his arm. I watch and feel nothing for Clutch. Whether or not he's lying or telling the truth this is the way of the club, its brotherhood before everything. I was just hoping to get some information before we got to this point.

"So Clutch, now that you're feeling a bit lighter. Is there anything else you'd like to say?"

"Good lucking finding the informant, assholes. I fear no fucking death."

A loud gunshot echoes as Clutch's head jerks hard to the right and blood spills from the large exit wound of Blade's glock.

"What the fuck, Blade? We needed to get him to talk."

"There wasn't shit that traitor had to tell us; burn the bodies and get the prospects out here with a truck to clean up the mess. Have them scrap the bikes and we'll take the parts. Get it done or get the fuck out of my club." I don't argue; Blade's lost and needs to collect his shit before I even try and talk some logical sense to him. It's been a long night and this shit has my adrenaline at full capacity. I need to get home and see my girl. There's nothing better than fucking after something this deep.

Chapter Six

Piper

"So did Blade really walk in on you naked in the club? Do you not know better than that, Piper? I can't believe he didn't literally cut Switch's dick off right there." We both know the possibility of that happening in the beginning was very real, but luckily time has been on my side with this.

My attraction to Switch has only grown and it's obvious he's had a connection with me since the first day we met.

"Yes, I did and it was fucking fantastic, so don't hate on me for finally getting Switch to give in to me. I was beginning to think I was losing my fucking charm." She laughs loudly as I flop down on the couch next to her.

"How long will the guys be gone?" I turn to her, impatiently wanting her to tell me how quick they are on these jobs, but we both know sometimes it's the next day before they ride back in.

"Not sure. I don't like how Blade was when he left here. I know that means someone is about to seriously pay for some shit they've done." She looks worried and I have to admit for the first time I'm actually thinking about their safety out there. I've never been around when they rush out and to be honest it's unnerving to watch the aggression on my brother's face. Seeing him like that made me see just what he could be capable of.

"I know. We could drink until they get back to pass the time." She smiles at me knowing I'll win this and we'll end up drinking, but she has to put up some sort of fight and be the voice of reason. "Don't even try to tell me no."

She laughs loudly at me as she walks to the liquor bottles behind the bar. "I'm not saying no. I know better than that. Besides, it'll only get us ready for the guys when they return. If Switch is anything like Blade after a night like this, you're in for one hell of a treat tonight. Consider this your warning." I stop mid step and look at her curiously.

"Sex is great after a run. Just wait. Now drink up. Tonight we drink to new beginnings and fucking fantastic orgasms that hopefully will come to you as often as they do me." Her huge smile makes me happy and for once my heart is full knowing we're both in a position to be content with our love lives.

We both down the shot and set it down for another fill just as the door bursts open to the clubhouse bar and a bloody Blade and Switch both walk with aggression towards the bar. Blade walks behind the bar and Switch stands on the other side leaning against it. The intensity is unreal and I honestly don't know whether to say something or just watch them to see how this plays out. Blade grabs a bottle of whiskey from the private stock and pours two shots. He's staring down Switch as he does everything. He finally sets the bottle down and takes both shots for himself.

Neither of them break eye contact the entire time. "Lock it all down tonight. I'm out. I'm driving Six home. We can deal with this shit tomorrow." I can feel there's tension between the two of them, and judging by the amount of blood they're both covered in and the shirts they just stripped out of, I'm willing to wait it out and get it out of Switch after Blade and Tori leave.

Switch fires a comment that makes the room halt to a silence. "You're gonna pull that bottle out and take two shots and not pour me one after the run we just had? I had your back the entire time, even when you didn't want to listen to a damn thing I had to say."

"You follow the orders I give you. There isn't room for second guessing when we're on a run; it's life or death out there and my job is to get shit done and do what's best for the club."

"All I'm saying is he could have said more and you let your anger and hatred blind that."

"When you're wearing my patch, then you can fucking question me. Until then we do as planned." This is enough of this I'm not going to sit here and watch my brother and the man I've fallen for decide to try and beat the hell out of each other over this.

"That's enough, you're not going to come in here and start a fucking fist fight with each other over whatever the hell just happened out there." Blade shoots me a death glare telling me to mind my own business, but he should damn well know better than that. I'm not going to sit here silently while this goes on in front of me. I grab the bottle of whiskey from in front of Blade and grab all four shot glasses and fill them. "You're both here alive and you have us, so man the fuck up, swallow your damn pride and take these shots like men and get the fuck over it."

Both Switch and Blade are now staring at me blankly like they just saw a ghost. Neither of them object and reach for their glass while Tori and I follow.

"Here's to alcohol, making dicks soft when they try to be hard."

"I thought this was my club, but apparently this is a fucking sorority house." Blade drops his shot glass and begins to walk away.

"Evan, stop being crazy. That's your little sister and she cares about you. I care about you and we've been worried about you boys all night. Can't you just chill the fuck out and have a drink with us? You guys can resolve all of this tomorrow and you know I can take care of your over-aggressive ass later."

"Alright, this is bullshit. Six. I fucking get it, I'll handle all of this my own way tomorrow. Switch, catch." Blade throws a towel from under the bar and shoots him a look that says this isn't over, but I'll let it slide for now. "It's a bar towel but at least you can clean that dried blood off your face. If we're gonna drink, let's fucking drink. I need a few before she tries to do some crazy shit and tie my ass up." He finally smirks toward Tori and I try to feel better about where they're at in all of this, but something still doesn't sit right with me.

"Jesus Blade, didn't you make the rule about not bringing up sex lives around me? Or do you want to start this game?" I try to lighten up the situation even more, but his look doesn't follow how I hoped he'd react.

"Talk about fucking around and I'll make you leave. I'll send you away from this fucking place like I should have in the first place." His words only infuriate me and this is the point where yet again I'm going to put him in his place.

"Excuse me. Try to make me move and you'll have one hell of a fight on your hands. I've already made it very clear that you do *not* control me." I slam my shot glass down and walk away from the bar. *Who does he think he is?* And what is it going to take to get him to take me seriously?

"This is my fucking club. People need to remember that shit." Evan swipes his hand across the bar, sending all the shot glasses to the floor. He keeps walking until he slams the front door behind him.

I watch Tori's look become even more frustrated before she stands to follow him. "I'll see you tomorrow, Pipes. I have to handle his cranky ass." She squeezes me tight in a hug and I can feel a shift in the air as I watch Switch over her shoulder.

He's watching my face. Watching me. His eyes never leave me, even when Tori tells him goodbye.

He's standing, yet leaning against the bar as he looks like he's waiting for me to come to him. I sit on the arm of the couch and exhale in frustration. This night has been pure fucking chaos and now he's sitting here looking at me like he's about to attack me. And sadly, I can't even think about sex right now. I need a damn minute to clear my head.

Fuck. He just ran his hand through his hair and flashed that sexy as hell smile in my direction. Yeah, I won't last long being upset with him looking like that.

Chapter Seven

Switch

Finally.

They're fucking gone.

I can't take another minute of this, I need to feel her now. The tension in my body can only be relieved in two ways. Either fighting or fucking. And right now fucking her is all I can think about.

"Woman, you're coming with me." I walk over to Piper and pick her up and toss her over my shoulder. She smacks my ass and I don't even try to stop her from kicking and cussing at me. It only takes her a few seconds before she's reaching around my waist and trying to grab my cock. I smile as I continue walking. She's feisty as fuck with a mouth on her that matches my own. I couldn't imagine anything less than that from a woman I'd be with.

She grips my dick through the denim and slides her hand over it a few times. She can play her games because she knows she'll get so much more of that from me. I owe her so much for the weeks of teasing she's tortured me with.

This only encourages me to grab a handful of ass and squeeze tight; of course I let a finger slide into her shorts just to torture her even further. “Switch. Stop. Seriously. I can walk my damn self.” She can consider that a reminder of who’s in charge here and I think she does because she gets real quiet as I continue to walk us through the house.

We make it up the stairs and into the shower when I turn the water on us both. Yes, we’re fully clothed, but sometimes peeling wet clothes off of a sexy body is something I like to do.

I let her slide down and lock herself around my waist as the water consumes us both. She begins to trace the music notes on my chest and locks her eyes on mine. I can read her; she wants to know it all. Every detail of what made me who I am, but right now isn’t the time. I need to be inside her. I need to feel her wrapped around me as I fuck her over and over.

I push her back against the wall with my kiss and rip her shirt open down the front. Her perfect tits are exposed as water runs down and over them. I watch the water trail a path over her body and imagine running my tongue over each and every one of the streams sliding over her body.

She slides her fingernails down my chest then reaches for my belt. I watch as her eyes shift and desire floods her face. She’s looking into my eyes the entire time she works my belt open and something hits me deep inside as she bites her lip and grinds against me once my pants fall open. She's sexy as fuck and I love that she doesn't try to hold back with me. She's bold and takes what she wants and luckily we want the same thing right this very moment.

I grab her ass and hold her against me as I quickly kick my pants off. They fall somewhere in the shower with us, but I don't give a shit where. I've never craved someone as badly as I do her and I want nothing in the way of getting to her.

I let her to her feet only to kneel down and strip her tiny shorts from her body. I slide her legs over my shoulders and lift her off the floor. She arches her back perfectly and leans back against the wall as I rise to my feet, giving me the perfect angle to fully taste her as she straddles my face.

Her wetness begins to flow as my tongue works her. She tastes every bit as good as I've been imagining and it's making me fucking crazy. Her grip on my hair is tight and her moans are loud as I send her into an orgasm. Her release takes over her entire body until she's left in her own euphoria as she leans heavily against the wall.

I look up to watch everything about her. She's gorgeous. I should know, I've watched her for weeks as she strutted around in front of me and then continued to torture me in my dreams as I slept. Her hair is drenched and partially stuck to her face. Her breathing is deep, causing her tits to move and my dick to beg for some attention. Her lips are swollen from my kiss and her body is flushed from the heat of the shower. She couldn't be sexier than she is right now.

I guide her down as she runs her hand through my hair and pulls me in for a kiss. She wants this, all of this with me. Her kiss is rough and demanding, only encouraging me to be the same. I pull her hair back and then grip her throat with my other hand. She stops to look at me as we both breathe heavily against each other.

Our chemistry is like a wildfire consuming everything in its path. I've never felt like this and that shit should fuck with me, but it doesn't. For once in my life I feel like everything is right where it needs to be.

I press myself against her as she runs her hands over my back. I can feel her fingers tracing the muscles in my back, taking in every ridge like she's burning it to memory. My skin erupts with sensation as she continues to explore and I realize just how long it's been since I let a woman appreciate me like this. This really isn't something I let happen with other women.

She lets her nails graze over my shoulders again and my dick decides I'm done being patient. I'm fucking rock hard watching her and I can't take another second of this. I fill my hands with her ass and pull her closer to me. She slides her leg up over my hip, allowing me to enter her and I start to slide into her slowly. *Fuck, she feels amazing.*

She grips tight on the back of my neck and pulls herself against me as she feels me thrust inside her. The feeling of arousal is consuming me. She's consuming me. Her tight grip on my cock only intensifies my desire to fuck her senseless.

Fuck. I need to make her come for me.

I crave it. I crave watching her take me in and lose her mind as she accepts all that I'll do to her.

Her eyes meet mine and she never looks away as I thrust in and out of her. "Ah. You feel so fucking good." She blinks as my deep voice spreads across her lips and my tongue slides over my bottom lip. That's all it takes for her to dive in for another rough kiss as we both fight for air while the water falls over us.

We move against each other with desperation to get closer even though it's not physically possible. She's fucking perfect and I'm not sure I'm ready for all she brings into my life, but right now, in this very moment I know I want to try. She's blasted her fucking way through my wall even though I resisted her many times. I wonder why I even bothered trying to hold her back. I knew the first day I met her that she was a persistent woman that would end up getting what she wanted; I guess I just figured she'd get tired of me rejecting her. Now there's no fucking way I'll ever deny her again. She wants my dick, she fucking gets it. I'll give it to her in any way she wants.

I let one of her legs free as I brace myself against the wall. She stands shorter than me like this, so I spin her leg over and thrust myself hard into her from behind. I can tell I'm deeper by the response her body gives me and the way her hands clasp to the tile wall of the shower. Her moans of pleasure fill my ears and only help to fulfill my sexual cravings.

I grip her hip with one hand and take a fistful of hair with the other. She arches her back and looks over her shoulder with complete satisfaction on her face. She loves me rough. "Oh, fuck yesssss." I can't hold back my appreciation any longer. "Piper, I love when you're about to fucking lose it. I can feel you clamping down on my dick. Come on baby, let me hear you."

She begins to moan louder. She turns to spread her hands over the wall again and I take notice of her gorgeous back again. Her ink intrigues me, but not enough to stop and trace it right now. I'll save that for another day… or night.

I decide to pull her against me and let the sight of her tits under my tatted arm and my grip on her send me so close to the fucking edge. Her entire body stiffens and I can feel the walls of her pussy enclose on my dick right before she releases.

I don't even give her a chance to regain herself before I thrust deep and hard into her again. I want this moment to last forever with her. I need to consume her in the deepest way, just like she has me. She needs to crave everything I have to give her and tonight I have so much more.

I slow myself and make each thrust more intense as I rock her G-spot every time. She begins to say my name and before I'm done, she's screaming it. I can't get enough of this; I'm drowning in the sound of her appreciative voice as she continues to whimper each time I enter her.

I pull out only to have her wrapped around my waist again. I don't let her lean against the wall this time, I want to have her completely at my mercy. I grip her ass tight as I begin to move her up and down on my cock. She feels amazing in my arms like this and her eyes are taking in my determination to make her feel me in every way. Each time I slide her slowly up and down on my length I can feel our connection getting stronger. This is so much more than a fuck and I can tell she feels it too.

I ignore that feeling and thrust deep into her over quickly, trying to make her scream again. “Switch, I’m ready. I need to please you the way you’ve pleased me.” *Fuck.* Her words are like a drug to me. She slides down my body and drops to her knees, gripping my thighs as she does.

She works her hands up and down the length as she licks the head of my hard cock. Before I know it she’s working her way down the shaft with her tongue and then pulling back to take me into the back of her throat.

Fuck. She swallows hard on me, making me feel my own release surface with a fury. I pull back knowing I’m so close, but she continues to stroke me hard until she’s aiming my dick so that my cum lands on her chest.

She gives me an instant look of gratification in what she’s done for me. This girl has me fucking crazy. The look on her face right now is something I never want to forget. She’s sexy and her confidence only makes her more irresistible to me.

I pull her to her feet and let her wash herself first before I grab the bar of soap to slide it over her body. I find myself taking in every one of her curves and some of the detail in her ink.

After we both wash ourselves, she steps out of the shower and grabs us both a towel. Her eyes skate down my body and I let her look without even considering turning away. My dick is still standing at attention and I have a feeling that won't be changing anytime soon with her around. "Meet me downstairs, I want another drink before I go to bed with you." Fuck if I'm going to argue with that kind of demand; shit, I might take that ass behind the bar when I get there if she keeps that shit up.

She leaves me to the steamy bathroom and I exhale deeply. My mind begins to float over the bullshit that happened tonight and even though fucking is a great release for stress, I'm still feeling like a shitstorm is brewing with Blade and the club. I'll need to handle some shit in the morning with him before he gets out of hand. It's my fucking job to make sure he stays level, and tonight he was not.

I wrap my towel around my waist and choose not to even bother with clothes. They'll just be coming off soon anyway. I smile as I think about all the shit I've imagined doing to her and now that I can, I have to say that shit excites me. She'll be up for anything and I plan to have some fucking fun with her.

I walk up behind her and grab her waist to pull her tight against me and fuck if she doesn't feel perfect pushing that firm ass into me, instantly causing my blood to rush. I run my hands up her body and caress her tits over her thin t-shirt. Sliding my hand over her neck and through her hair, I move her head to the side and breathe heavy on her neck.

I feel her body pulse for me as she exhales a moan and grabs my hand to slide it down her chest and stomach until I feel the heat between her legs. There's no way I could ever get enough of this. I start stroking her clit before I let my fingers enter her. Her body is still hungry for my hard cock and who am I to ever say no to her again?

She pulls my hand from her and turns toward me, looking as hungry as she always has at me. She's not looking like I've just fucked her senseless in the shower. My intensity spikes again and I lift her ass onto the bar only taking a step back to kiss down her legs. I eventually run my tongue over her clit and suck it into my mouth, causing her to grab a hold of my hair and pull it hard. *Fuck. The sound of her moans turns me on. Her grip turns me on. Her taste turns me on. Shit, everything she does turns me on.*

I need her to be as rough with me as I am her. I brush my beard up to her stomach as I pull her body close to mine and stand to my feet. She's sitting on the bar and

I'm thankful my height is just perfect for what's about to happen. Sliding my hard cock over her entrance a few times before I thrust deep into her is just a warning for her to prepare herself.

She doesn't break eye contact with me until I draw back. She wraps her arms around my neck to pull herself up to watch me thrust into her again. I look down to see what she's seeing and fuck me if that isn't the sexiest thing I've seen. "You like watching yourself get fucked by me, don't you Piper." Before she answers, I thrust into her again. She tosses her head back and closes her eyes tight as I slide her against the bar with each thrust of my hips.

I hold her ass in my hands and squeeze. "Don't forget this ass is mine." She nods as I fill her with my hard cock once again.

"Fuck me harder, Switch." Her words send me into an uncontrollable frenzy to give her exactly what she's asking for. I go harder and deeper with each and every stroke, feeling her reach a climax again and again. Fuck, I love pleasing my girl this way.

Shit, I just said it. *My girl.*

I pick her up and take her up against the back wall of the bar, her nails dig into my back and it has me dying to reach my own release yet again. "I want to feel you come inside me." Her words are like electricity coursing through my veins and it takes me no time to reach my own climax. I feel her tighten around me and watch her body quiver before wetness runs down between us. I pull her in for a kiss and feel her tongue tangle with mine as I pull out of her and slide her off of the bar. and turn her back around.

"Fuck Piper, you have no idea what you do to me." I exhale, trying to catch my breath as she slides down my body. She just smiles and adjusts her tiny t-shirt to cover her body, grabs my hand and leads me back to the bedroom.

We make it up to my room and both crawl into bed completely naked. The feeling of her warm skin against mine as she has her left arm and leg sprawled over me has me feeling more comfortable than I'd like to admit. Everything about this feels right, and I don't ever want it to end.

For now, I'll just enjoy these moments while they last; maybe I can have something stable even with the club and all the other hell going on. She falls asleep quickly and I continue to think about how the world is perfect right this very moment, even if all hell is going to break loose when I talk to Blade about the shit that went down tonight.

Chapter Eight

Piper

Fuck, it's early.

I look over to see Switch still asleep; even passed out this man is gorgeous. No wonder I can't keep my hands off him. I might just have to wake him up and tease the fuck out of him for a bit just as payback. It's so crazy that all this happened; I still can't grasp the concept of having him in my life.

I need coffee first before today starts; I'm sure Evan will be here soon barking orders and demanding all sorts of things. I'll just borrow Switch's shirt again; he can have it back when he rips it off me.

The kitchen is quiet; actually everything is really quiet. This isn't unusual for this place this early, not even in the slightest. I keep looking just to make sure no one is here and just didn't announce themselves. I don't like surprises. The garage is empty with the exception of the two cars pulled in and all of the parts scattered about from the guys working out there yesterday.

Suddenly I hear a faint roar of a motorcycle in the distance. "Must be Evan," I mumble to myself as I reach down to pull my shirt down a little lower. I'm sure he won't approve of me wearing this around the clubhouse, but I'm not going to listen to his big brother bullshit this morning.

Today nobody can bring me down from this high, not even Evan. I feel amazing and the way Switch treated me last night was more than I could've imagined. His touch was demanding and caring at the same time. I could see how he felt through his dark brown eyes as he watched me come undone over and over in his arms.

He's falling for me, whether he wants to admit it or not. I'll let him pretend this is just a sexual thing between us until he's ready to admit otherwise.

I walk back upstairs to grab a pair of shorts as I hear the rumble get even closer to the house. Glancing over at Switch, I can't help but smile as I watch him stir and reach for me across the bed. He looks up just as I walk closer and I instantly wish like hell I could just tell Evan to leave so I can spend the day with Switch in this bed.

"My brother is here; I'll just tell him you're still sleeping so you can get some rest." He nods at me just before he lays his head on my pillow and pulls it in tight against his chest. I decide I'm going to rush Evan away from here and make my way back into his arms before we both have to leave for the day.

Tiptoeing down the stairs, I try to minimize the creaking sounds, expecting to see Evan by the bar. I'm actually surprised when he's not there. *Fuck. I need coffee.* I hear the door behind me open as I walk down the hall toward the kitchen.

I quickly turn to see a prospect startled when he sees me, so I just keep walking. "Mornin'. Looks like I'm early. Where's everyone else?" His squeaky little voice is oddly annoying and I almost tease him about it, but I choose to hold my tongue. I can tell he's nervous and most likely trying to prove himself to my brother and Switch.

I can see how they could be intimidating to most people, but I'm not one of those people. "Still in bed, I'd imagine." I can hear his footsteps following me into the kitchen. Choosing to ignore him, I begin to make some coffee.

He walks closer to me and I can see his boots next to my bare feet before I feel him grip my shoulder and cover my face with a dirty rag. The room goes dark instantly before I have the chance to realize what he's doing.

~~~~~~~~~~~~~~
~~~~~~~~~~~~~~

"Wake the fuck up, Bitch." The horrendous scent of disgusting breath slaps me in the face as I start to wake up. My arms are being pulled tight by metal chains and my shoulders are forced to stretch until I'm screaming in pain. I try to see who's near me, but I can't make out the dark silhouettes through my swollen eyes.

"Cut her clothes off. I want to see those tits." My insides are destroyed the second I hear his words. The next thing I hear is the sound of my clothes being cut from my body. They don't worry about making sure they don't cut me in the process and I can feel the burn of the blades as they pass over me. My shirt falls open and one of them grips the material with his hands and rips it off of me the rest of the way. My shorts follow.

"Fuck. I'm gonna love this one. No bra or panties… It's like she's begging for us to fuck her." Another voice comes from behind. I can count at least six men around me. Two holding the chains, the one in front of me, and the two that cut my clothes off.

I try to let my mind remember how I got here, but I have nothing. I can see junk cars and realize quickly that I'm in a salvage yard of some sort. Bright spotlights keep me from seeing anything very clearly, but at least I was able to make that part out.

My heart is beating out of control and my mind is spiraling into chaos as I imagine what they're going to do to me. I wish like hell Evan or Switch would walk up and kill each one of these fuckers right now, but I know I won't be that lucky.

The sound of a truck gives me hope, but when I hear the guys acknowledge another voice it ruins me. *Seven.* There's seven men and I'm tied up naked. There's really only one way this can go. The possibilities horrify me and being chained up restricts me from doing anything to get out of this situation.

I lose focus on what they're saying as I drift to my past and begin to relive the worst night of my life, up until tonight. Even though I know that night will be nothing compared to what's about to happen, it was the night my life changed forever.

One of the chains slips before it's yanked back, pulling my arm even higher. The other guy follows his lead and I'm now literally standing on the tip of my toes trying to stay steady.

A rough hand slides around my side from behind and grips my right nipple hard before he rips his fingers away. The pain of feeling like my nipple was ripped off causes me to make a sound and then I can hear the rest of the guys walking toward me.

"I told you to leave her the fuck alone until I'm done with her. I'll let you have my leftovers…" He moves in close to my face and I try to recognize him, but I can't. "If I leave any." He slides his hand down my chest and over my nipples as he finishes talking.

I try to take in everything. This won't be like the last time; I'll find this fucker. He's wearing a black shirt, black jeans, and boots. His beard is unkept and if I had to guess his age, I'd say he's in his forties. His characteristics are like so many of the guys so I'll need to look for tattoos or something that sets him apart. If I focus on that, maybe I'll be able to get through this.

"You Blade's sister?" He grips my throat as he questions me and gets so close to my face that his nose is almost touching mine.

I nod my head yes, even though I know he already knows this. There's no reason to lie about it and piss him off even further.

"I need to remind him of something. And I just decided, you're going to deliver my message." I look at his face close and see zero compassion. This man is hard and I instantly have to work to try to process what he's saying. My head is already trying to escape the situation and I know I need to remember everything I can.

"In fact, maybe I'll just call him and tell him myself. He might listen if I tell him with my dick buried inside his sister." I close my eyes knowing how much that will torture Evan. He will rage like never before and I can't stand the thought of him going through that.

"I can tell him for you, just tell me what you want and let me go." His hysterical laughter hits me in the face before he begins to walk around me, ducking under the chain on my left. His hand scrapes across my stomach and over my ass while he circles me before he slides it around the front of me and shoves his hand between my legs and his fingers inside me. The urge to vomit is strong and the need to kill is even stronger.

"You're not going anywhere. That tight little pussy will be tore up when we finish with you." He pulls me into his body, lifting me just enough that I can no longer touch the ground. His breath hits my ear and I work with everything in my body to take what he does and not lose it. I can feel my mind swirling as my body continues to try to separate me mentally, even though I'm fighting it for at least a few more minutes. I want to know who these fuckers are.

"You see. Your brother thinks he's some fucking god. He thinks he gets to decide when people live or die." He scrapes me as he pulls his hand away and drops me to dangle until my feet settle. I have to fight to get my footing once again and end up crying out just slightly. They all begin to laugh like they're fucking hungry to get a piece of me, which only causes me to go deeper into the darkness.

The burn on my back takes over everything in my mind as I feel him slice my back open while he talks. "There's seven of us. I'm going to leave you with a reminder."

I swallow as he takes the knife across the top of my back, then down from my right shoulder to the top of my ass. Blood begins to run instantly and my body pulls me into the numbness without any hope of me stopping it. I should be thanking my internal defense right now, but that would take logic, which I don't seem to have.

"Give me Blade's fucking phone number. I want him to hear this. Maybe now that fucker will listen to what I have to say." I close my mouth with his demand. I can't do this to Evan. Him knowing it happened will be bad enough. I don't really want him to hear me being tortured at his expense. I can't imagine a worse nightmare than if I had to listen to his reactions as all of this is happening.

"You're going to give me his number one way or the other. But if you want to close that fucking mouth, I'll give you reasons to open it." He forces his dirty fingers between my lips and pulls my jaw down. I open wider hoping to get my teeth into position to fight back, knowing it'll most likely only make this worse. He removes his hand quickly before I have the chance to lock my teeth down, then squeezes my cheeks together, forcing my mouth to open slightly.

He runs his lips over mine and my insides instantly twist as I fight back vomit. Fuck. I'd rather die than go through this again.

How can this be happening again? I thought it could never be worse than it was that night, but this seems to be an entirely new level of hell.

Switch

"Where the fuck is she?" I lean forward and ask Blade for the fucking third time.

"Maybe she needed some space after you stuck your damn dick in her." He leans back like he's annoyed that I've asked again.

"She couldn't get enough of me. If she's not at your house, then something is wrong." I can feel it. I remember her saying she was going to talk to Blade yesterday morning as I slept and he told me he wasn't the one who showed up at the house.

I've had a bad feeling and I can't fucking shake it. She's been begging to get me to bed and she wouldn't run from me after the night we had. She left her phone here and she would've had to have been picked up because her car is still at Blade's. It isn't like her to disappear for an entire fucking day and night.

"I can pull all the guys to look for her, but we both know my sister does what she wants. She may be in New York shopping for a fucking wedding dress for you to get married for all we know." I watch him run his hand down his face and over his beard as I try to decide how I want to handle these fucked up feelings I have.

"Get the guys in here. I want to ask them who was here this morning." I look to Beast for him to make the call. Blade leans forward as soon as the call ends and spreads his hands out on the table before he stands to talk to all of us.

"I handled Clutch last night. He spewed some bullshit about the club being poisoned by a traitor before I killed him. Who knows anything? Just remember I'll fucking kill anyone who lies to me but you have no fucking chance if you lie in this room." He begins to walk behind all of us as we sit at the table. It's just the officers in here right now, so just as expected, none of us respond with anything.

"I want ears on all the fuckers in this club. Until I tell you it's all good, we don't talk outside these closed doors about any club business. Trust no one." He's fully circled the room before he sits back down at the head of the table.

I know he's been talking, but my thoughts still seem to be on where in the hell Piper is. Watching Beast, I want for him to get any texts. When one finally comes, he looks over at me before he speaks up. "All members are on their way except one prospect who made a trip to see his parents today." I grip my fists and think about what I'd do if anything happened to her. The shit that's been going on around here lately has me on edge and ready to move the hell to the mountains to spare myself from half the bullshit like Blade did.

"I want every one of them talked to individually about this shit so it's going to be one long fucking night." Blade stands to leave the room and I look to each of the other guys around the table.

My phone vibrates and I answer it quickly even though I don't recognize the number.

"Hey Boss, this is Tank. I'm headed in like Beast said you wanted, but can't get ahold of Chewy. He's out at the salvage yard today. Do you want me to stop by and pick his lazy ass up?" Tank is a prospect that I've taken in as my own little project. He will make it into the club soon because I'm making sure of it.

"Yes. Get here as soon as you can. We'll start when you do." I hang up, frustrated that I'm having to deal with all this bullshit when I feel like I need to be looking for Piper.

Beast steps out of the room and leaves the door open. I can hear a few of the guys start to show up and they're all greeted with Blade's grumbly voice. "Have you seen my fucking sister?" At least he's starting to feel like it's something we need to focus on even if he's practically raging in the face of every one of the guys walking through that door, probably thinking they're all the leak in the club.

It's not long before he's dragging them all into the chapel to sit them down and interrogate each one. They all seem collected and innocent and it begins to piss me off. It's fucking getting dark and we need to get the hell out of this room and find her.

My phone vibrates and I look to see Tank calling again, so I pick up.

"Boss, there's someone at the salvage yard. I went dark as soon as I saw all the lights. There's at least five from what I can see. Do you want me to go in solo?"

"Someone is on our property without our knowledge… You fucking never go in solo." I start to make my way to the door before I end the call. Blade is on my heels along with Beast and the clubhouse door slams behind us before I say a word.

"Tank says we have company at the salvage yard. Chewy is off the grid and never checked out; we need to make a trip to see who's decided to stop by." Blade stands with his hand on his beard before he turns to look back at the row of bikes lined up in front of the house. I don't wait for him to decide if he's coming, stepping over my bike and firing up the engine before I look back to see both of them following suit.

I need to do something with this aggression before I fucking kill one of my own club guys thinking about where in the fuck Piper could be. The wind hits my face as I speed down the road with a rage that can only be explained as one similar to the way Blade acts every fucking time he's ready to kill a mother fucker.

We pull up next to Tank and kick off the lights at the top of the overlook. I can see the lights in the middle of the yard and men standing, but I can't make out how many or tell what they're doing.

"Do we go in guns blazing or get closer to see what's going on?" Tank begins to ask questions that I'm thinking to myself.

"We go in blazing. I don't fucking tip toe," Blade responds as he looks down at his phone. He puts it against his ear and I watch the insanity take over his face as he begins to listen.

"Touch her and I'll fucking cut your skin off one fucking inch at a time, starting with your god damn dick." My insides twist all to hell with his words because I know this call is about Piper.

I stand and pull the phone out of his hand not giving a fuck if he decides to lose his shit on me for it. This is about Piper, so it's my fucking business.

"I'll make you listen to her cries if you fuck with me. You have a load that's mine and it's time you learn your place when it comes to transporting my fucking guns." I can't place the name and hit speaker on the phone as I look down to see if the number showed a name. Of course it didn't. The voice sounds familiar, but fuck if I can tell who it is.

"Let me hear her." That's all I can get out. The look on Blade's face matches the way I feel when the fucker forces her to say something to us.

Fuck. Piper. How the fuck did I let this happen to you?

Chapter Nine

Piper

"Give me your brother's fucking number or I'll use a knife instead of my dick to fuck you." I glare into his eyes knowing he's not kidding. He doesn't give a shit if I live or die. I finally give in knowing this will devastate Evan, but I do it in hopes that he can somehow magically show up and save me like he did when we were kids. It's just fucked up that he'll have to hear all of this.

I whisper his number and watch him dial it with the largest grin on his face. The sound of Blade's voice pulls at me and I regret giving in immediately.

"There's only one question here… Do you want me to talk to you while I fuck your sister or should I let my guys have her first?" He doesn't get the chance to finish before I can hear Blade's voice roaring back at him.

Hands grip me from behind and I hear a zipper lowering before I feel a cock against my back. The leader points back at the guy behind me and he takes a step back. I don't know whether to be thankful that he stopped that or scared to death of what he has planned for me instead.

"I'll make you listen to her cries if you fuck with me. You have a load that's mine and it's time you learn your place when it comes to transporting my fucking guns." He's talking about firearms and that only verifies my instincts about who this guy is. I've been guessing that he's a big deal in another club, only making this scarier than just a random attack. This means war. I know my brother well enough to know he'll ruin his club to get revenge for something like this.

"Say something." He grips my face as he moves the phone closer and forces me to talk. I can hear Switch yell back as soon as I say the single word that came out of my mouth. The only word that keeps circling my head and has me more terrified than I've ever been in my life. '*Seven'*.

"Piper. Talk to me." He wraps his palm over my face to stop me from saying anything else, but makes me listen to Switch continue to talk with Blade yelling in the background.

"It's time I get paid some of what you cost me. How much do you think this pussy I have here is worth?" He takes the phone away from me and starts to take a few pacing steps in front of me before he walks around behind me. The sound of his zipper tells me my luck has run out and I swallow hard trying to prepare for what he's about to do. Tears fall down my cheeks and I squeeze my fists tight to remind myself that I'm still strong.

He slides between my legs and shoves inside me with a vulgar roughness. I'm instantly sent into the horrors of my own memories as I fall back to the last time this happened to me.

He pulls me back to reality every time he begins to talk and I hear Switch on the other end of the phone losing his shit. "Piper, baby. Listen to me. I'll fucking kill this mother fucker. Stay strong, I'm coming for you." The scum with his hands all over me tosses his phone to one of the other guys before he picks up his pace and goes even deeper as he lifts my legs, giving him complete access.

It takes everything in me to go numb and stay that way until he finally drops me. I don't even know how long it took him, but I don't even try to stand once he drops me. The torture of another set of hands spreads over my skin and I go black. This is the safest place for me to be.

Voices swirl around in my head as the rough texture of so many things scrapes over my skin. Hands. Knives. Zippers. Chains. All of them making it hard to keep down the poison stirring in my stomach.

Switch

"I heard the fucking chain scrape across the metal. They have her in the mother fucking yard." I don't say another word before my bike is roaring straight for the yard. I'm going to kill every one of these fuckers with my goddamn bare hands.

Before I can get to the bottom of the clearing, I see a truck hauling ass followed by two bikes. Blade zooms past me with Beast right on his ass when I slide to a stop for Piper.

My heart aches at the sight in front of me. Fuck. She's naked and blood is dripping from her lifeless body as she hangs with her arms spread tight by a chain on the fucking bars we use to torture the guys we bring here. I can't explain what's going through my mind as I race to hold her.

"Shit. Talk to me, Piper. I'm here baby." She doesn't move or help me as I lift her into one arm and work to release her from the chains with the other. My arms are covered in blood as I hold her against me and try to find where it's coming from. "Show me something. Come on." I yell into her face and begin to feel frantic when she doesn't respond to anything I say.

I take off running with her in my arms until I'm inside the shop. This fucking place is not clean enough for me to even find a solid place to lay her down, so I lay her on the hood of one of the cars someone's been working on. She doesn't move a fucking muscle and I fight to keep the insanity inside as I let my eyes look over her body.

She has blood and cuts all over her body, so bad that I can't tell where she's hurt more. The anger inside builds as I take it all in. "I will fucking skin these mother fuckers alive starting with their dicks, Piper. Please show me some fucking sign that you're with me." She shows me nothing. *Fuck.*

I reach for my phone and call Shadow. Before he has a chance to say hello I'm ordering him around. "Bring me a fucking truck to the salvage yard now. Someone has fucked up Piper bad."

"On my way." He barely lets me finish before he hangs up and I look back down at Piper hoping to see some sort of response. I finally find a half cluttered table and race to lay her down on it so I can see her closer. That fucking hood isn't working.

I can't stand what I'm seeing. How can this be the same woman that I held just this morning? I know she has to go to the hospital, but with all this blood everywhere, I just don't know how bad everything is. She still has yet to react to me, but I can see that she's breathing. I pull my flannel shirt off and drape it over her body and begin to talk to her once again.

"Piper please, baby. Can you hear me? I'm here for you." I squeeze her hand and she doesn't react at all. Nothing I do gets any sort of response from her and I begin to flip the fuck out as I look at her and see more cuts and even further swelling from the obvious beating she endured. Her arms are marked heavily from the chains and her eyes are nearly swollen shut. My screams of outrage and frantic desperation fill the shop as I wait impatiently for someone to get here.

Shadow finally pulls up with the truck and I meet him outside with her in my arms. Blade and Beast will deal with the guys if they can get to them before all the fuckers get away. If not, we'll find them. I'll make it my last mother fucking mission to wipe them off of this planet if it's the last thing I do.

"Holy shit." Shadow jumps out from the truck and opens the back door for me to slide her into the back seat. I sit in the back with her and feel the wetness of the blood on her back soaking me even further.

Shadow starts out driving like a bat out of hell. "Chill the fuck out. I'm ripping her fucking skin here." She needs steady and I know he's just trying to hurry, but the more I have to grip onto her, the more beat up she's going to be after all of this. Her cries gut me and make me feel like fucking shit forever letting her out of my sight.

Fuck. This pisses me off. How in the hell did this happen to her? Who in the fuck was it that came to the house this morning and how in the fuck did they get her to go with them? I normally don't let shit like this get by me and I know I did this time. She had me so damn distracted and I let my guard down.

I continue to beat myself up about her condition the entire way to the hospital. Shadow calls in a few minutes ahead of us arriving, so they're waiting with a gurney when we pull up. It takes some hustle to keep up with the doctors as they race her through the halls and nurse stops me to see if I need help because of all the blood on me.

They shove me out of the way in the room, actually allowing me in, but not anywhere near as they begin to work on her. The chaos of the night flashes over me as I watch them try to clean her up in hopes of seeing where the real injuries are. They turn her on her side and the doctor on that side shakes his head before he tells the nurse to clear the room.

"Not a fucking chance. I'm staying. I'll stand back here, but you're not getting me out of here." The doctor meets me with a glare that turns into an understanding when he sees my own. Luckily he has decided I'm not worth the battle and continues to work on her without focusing on me being in the room.

They pull the shirt from her body and I become even more outraged thinking of anyone hurting her at all, let alone how she is right now. An overwhelming desire to kill someone continues to take over and I have to work like hell to keep it at bay and stay calm. The last thing this place needs is me losing my shit and causing a fucking scene when most of them are rushing to work on Piper.

She still hasn't moved or reacted to anything they're doing to her. Her body has to be in shock and I just hope like hell she went into a safe place within her head before those fuckers hurt her this bad. I hear one of the doctors say she's going to need blood because she's lost so much.

He looks close at her back before he looks over at me and questions. "Seven? Does that mean anything to you?"

"No. Other than she said it on the phone when I was trying to get to her. I had no idea what it meant." I still don't and can only imagine that it means there were seven of them which only makes me crazier inside when I think about it.

“She has the number seven cut into her back. I need to do a rape kit and a few places need stitches. She’s going to hurt for a few days, but other than that we need to let her rest and see what happens.” I stand silently as they continue doing what they’re trained to do while I plot doing what I’ve been trained to do.

She’s still lifeless and for the first time in years I find myself actually saying a prayer. I just need for her to wake up and tell me who I need to kill.

“Can you please step outside while we do the rape kit? The patient deserves her privacy in this situation.” I look down at the tiny nurse trying to reason with me. She knows this was a far-fetched request, but I get that she’s just doing her job. I just can’t leave her. I refuse to.

“I’ll turn around and that’s the best I can do. I’m not leaving this room until she does.” The nurse nods at me quickly as if she expected that response. I consider this a compromise and turn around. My ears are at full alert as I listen for any information I can get as they continue their examination.

“No.” Piper cries out half coherent and I can’t handle it any longer. I move to be next to her as they swab and study between her legs for evidence. Gripping my own fist in a death grip isn’t making this any easier to watch. She shakes her head and says no quietly again before the doctor finishes and I reach for her hand and lean over to talk to her. She has to be able to hear me.

"Baby. I'm here. The doctor is almost done and I'm taking you home the second he is." She moves her head again, but she still hasn't opened her eyes.

"Please don't." She begins to shake her head even more and the doctor steps away from her. I know he hurried during that exam, but the truth of it is, I don't need his evidence to handle this. Justice will be met for her and I'll search until I go to my death bed to make sure of it if that's what it takes.

The nurse covers her and begins to clean her arms and legs. She's almost unrecognizable and it's killing me to see her like this. Blade is going to lose his shit when he sees her and I can't wait to watch the determination in his face when he instantly decides the fate of the men responsible for this.

The nurse finishes cleaning her up, but she's still so swollen and red that I'm afraid to touch her when they actually move us to a room. I sit next to her in a chair and hold one of her hands and simply watch her. She's still out of it and in a way that's a good thing. She needs to rest and honestly I don't know what I'd be able to say to her right now if she was awake. My anger is consuming every bit of my being and I can feel the rage building inside me even more as I look at the injuries that remain after the blood has been wiped clean.

I glance at my phone and there's still no call or text from Blade, so I can only imagine the shit they got into. I decide to call Tori and have her come to support Piper. "Tori, I need you to come to the hospital. It's Piper. She's alive, but she's going to need us both when she wakes up."

"What in the hell, Switch. What happened?" I can hear her moving around quickly as she begins to question me. I know there's no great way to tell her what I know, so I decide to make her come here before I break all of this to her. For one thing that's the safest thing to do for Tori's sake as well.

"I'll tell you everything when you get here. Who's with you?" I know Blade has her covered, I just can't think straight as to who it would be.

"Yes, Sarge is here."

"Have him bring you. Consider yourself stuck to a bodyguard until we tell you otherwise."

"Blade already called to tell me that. What the fuck is going on?" She's scared and I know she can tell this is bad, but I can't talk about it over the phone.

"I have to go. I'll talk to you when you get here." I hang up before she has a chance to ask another question. This shit is fucked up and I don't want to deal with Tori having a damn break down before she's here for me to watch over. That's something I'll always do for Blade, or any of the guys in the club. I'm hoping Tori can get Piper to wake up and talk to us together. They've been best friends for years and maybe her voice will snap Piper out of it. She'll no doubt be here as quick as she can.

I look over at Piper's face again. Her eyes begin to shift under her lids and I decide to try to talk to her once again. "Piper. Can you hear me?" She squeezes my hand and starts to open her eyes.

She mumbles the word Seven once again and my skin erupts with enough adrenaline to kill a thousand people.

Seven. What the fuck is Seven? The only thing I can think it means is seven men and then that's not even comprehensible. I continue to torture myself by imagining the torture she's endured and let it fuel me. Not that I need any more fuel.

Chapter Ten

Piper

My body hurts everywhere. I'm afraid to open my eyes and I begin to feel nauseous the second I let myself remember what happened.

The darkness of the hell I've been trapped in feels safer than facing the reality of what will go on once I open my eyes. Here I don't have to talk about it. It's over. What's done is done. If I stay right here in this state, I don't have to deal with people as they try to cope with what happened to me.

I can hear Switch. There was a day I'd have done anything to have him with me, but today I feel different. I don't want him to see me like this. I'm ruined.

"Can you hear me?" He speaks softly even though I can hear the anger in his voice. I know this has to be hard for him to deal with, which is why I don't want him here.

Forcing my eyes to open, I begin to move my legs only to stop right away. Fuck. It all hurts.

He moves closer to me and doesn't say a word. His eyes say enough. It's pity I see all over his face. He feels sorry for me and I want to fucking come out of this bed and scream at him, but I can't.

"Stop. Don't look at me." My voice sounds terrible and I start to feel myself get even more upset when he doesn't listen. "Please go."

"I'm not leaving you." He responds quickly and I begin to feel the chaos caving in on me. I turn away from him and start crying as I try to find a way out of this claustrophobic conversation.

"I can't deal with this. Please just leave." This time it comes out as a scream. I want him to leave. I need him to stop looking at me like he feels sorry for me and I wish like hell he didn't know what I just went through. How am I supposed to look at anyone again after all of this?

"Piper, stop. I'm not fucking leaving you." His refusal only makes me crazier. My yelling has the doctors rushing into the room and the last thing I remember is the sting of the shot before I relax and go back to sleep.

The shift of my hand and the soreness in my arm only reminds me that it wasn't just a nightmare. It really happened. "She was strung up on the fucking bar and I don't know who the fuck did this. I just know they signed their death wish the second they touched her." I can hear Switch and Tori talking. I try to stay calm and accept that they know pieces of what I went through, even if I don't remember all the details myself.

My heart begins to race as they continue to talk, so I make a movement to let them know I'm awake. Tori's scent invades my senses and her soft hands wrap around both of mine immediately.

"Fuck, Piper. I'm here." That's all she says. That's all she needs to say. I know she's here for me and always has been, but there's just somethings she can never understand, even if she tries. Just like I'll never comprehend everything that she's been through in her life. Words aren't strong enough to describe what we've been through in our lives.

Her slight squeeze on my shoulders hurts, but in a way it reminds me to continue feeling. Right now I'm drawn to the numbness swirling around inside my head. It's just easier that way.

I don't look at Switch. I can't. I don't want to see the way he looks at me. Before there's time for anything else to run through my mind, Blade busts through the door, moving as if death walks beside him. He's lost all touch with reality. I don't know how, but I can sense it as if it's the only thing I can feel in the room. The look on his face says everything he's not as the room fills with a heavy silence. He moves straight for me and doesn't let his eyes falter from taking in my appearance and every single one of my visible injuries.

"I have one of those fuckers and I'll get the rest of them. Tell me what you remember." He looks down at me with guilt all over his face. Guilt and disgust. It hits me deep inside the longer he looks at me. I try to take a deep breath, but can't with everyone staring at me like this.

"I don't know anything. I can't remember details." Blade desperately watches me like he wants me to keep talking, but he's gutted that I can't. I have nothing else to say, even though I wish like hell I could tell him who did this to me.

"Stop it right now. Quit looking at me like you feel sorry for me. I can't stand this. Either fix your fucking faces or get out. Don't you think it's bad enough to feel the like the filth I do? I don't need you looking at me like this for the rest of my life." I shift in the bed and squirm in pain as I do.

They all stand and try to look away to correct themselves. "I know this is awkward and strange, but for fuck's sake, I need to deal with all of this before I can handle all of you. Will you all please go?"

"Not a chance in hell." Switch is louder than Blade this time and I look at him through my swollen eyes and try to make him understand what I need from him. He's just like my brother and there's really only one way to get him to leave this room. I know what I need to do.

"Go find the fuckers who did this to me. Leave me here with Tori and let me heal. I can't stand you guys in here. You're too heavy in this room and I just can't fucking deal with that right now." He walks slowly to the side of the bed and I can tell he's thinking about what I'm asking.

"I'll be back as soon as I find them. Sarge is standing post outside the door and he has strict orders not to let anyone in." I nod quickly, agreeing so he'll leave and the hardest part is not turning away when he leans over to kiss me.

I want to want his kiss. It's just right now, I don't want anything except rest.

The guys leave and Tori looks at me with a serious stare on her face as she sits down on the bed next to me and lays down the law. "Rest. I'm going to stay with you and there's not one fucking thing you can say to get me to leave." I close my eyes knowing she's not joking in the slightest because that's exactly what I'd do if it was her lying in this bed.

The next thing I know it's daylight outside and I wake up to Tori sleeping next to me in the small hospital bed. She's holding my hand in hers and doesn't move until the door opens and the nurse barges in to take my vitals. "Looks like the doctor is releasing you this morning. I'll be working on your paperwork and he'll be in to see you shortly." She leaves as quick as she came in and Tori gets up quickly.

"What can I get you?" She starts to fuss over me again and I have to give it to her like I always have. Straight up honesty.

"I need you to treat me the same as you did yesterday." She looks at me sadly and I know she's going to struggle with this, but it's what I need.

"I'll do what I can. I just want to make sure you're ok."

"I'm not sure how I'll get there, but I will." I edge off the bed and let my feet touch the ground. It takes me a minute to walk across the room by myself, but I manage it. Tori gives this to me. It's just a small gesture showing she understands I need to do this for me.

I close the door to the bathroom and stop dead in my tracks in front of the mirror. It takes me gripping the sink to hold myself up as I glimpse at my face and take in all of the bruises. "I don't even look like me." Tori hears me talking and speaks through the closed door.

"Did you say you needed something?" I lower my gown and uncover more bruises. Bandages cover my back and I can't see what's under them, but I can feel that most of it feels tight and hurts as I move. When I don't respond, she opens the door. She looks at me reacting to the way I look and must see the feeling of disgust written all over my face.

I don't fight her when she wraps her arms around my neck and pulls me against her. Small flashes of that night continue to torture my mind and I'm fighting like hell to get past the way I feel inside as she holds me. She doesn't release me until we hear the doctor enter the room.

"How are you feeling today?" He asks me the impossible question. I feel disgusting. Dirty. Ruined. Damaged. Shredded into a million pieces only to be tossed on the ground to blow away in the wind. How else can I describe what I'm going through?

"I've been better," I respond and make my way back to the bed. Tori stays in the bathroom and closes the door. The doctor sits beside me and begins to go over everything.

"Your cuts need to be kept clean, especially on your back. You'll need to have the stitches removed in ten days or so. One of the standard medications we give is an emergency contraception used to prevent pregnancy from that point on. I want you to know there is a slight chance that you could be pregnant, but we won't know for sure for until a few days pass and we can test you." My mind goes insane at what he's saying and I can't even fathom being pregnant after all of this.

Tori opens the door and there's no doubt she heard everything he just said, but she does a good job of going with the flow of the room and keeping her reaction to a minimum for my sake.

Jesus. I feel like a damn fragile shell of myself as I think of everything that's happened and what this all means for me as I'll try to put all of this behind me. The real question is, can I do this with Switch, Tori, and my brother all huddled around me the entire time, reminding me daily that I've been through hell?

Switch

"Tell me what the fuck you know." I stop Blade right outside her door. He starts to walk around me before I stop him again. "Right the fuck now, Blade."

"We'll fucking talk outside. You know the goddamn rules." His angry response tells me this is going to be one fucked up situation. I follow him without another word and wait until he lights up a cigarette in the parking lot before I expect him to start talking.

"A fucking prospect of ours took her. He's at the yard being held until I tell them to move him." He takes a few steps each way as he talks and I just wait for the part where he tells me who else is behind all of this. "He's playing games and I'm headed to make him talk. Figured you'd want in on it because honestly, I want to kill him with just the possibility of him touching her." His voice cracks before he stops talking to smoke again and I have to make myself breathe in to calm the emotions that start to take over.

It'll be hard to rein in all of this anger and wait for him to talk. The possibility of him taking the information to his grave is huge but hell can't hide his soul. I'll get my answers and he'll suffer and beg for death before I'm finished with him.

"Beast is still working to find the other fuckers that did this, but for now I say we go deal with the piece of shit at the yard."

He throws his leg over his motorcycle and I call Shadow over to drive me. He just walked out a few minutes ago, I'm sure ready to serve some paybacks for the shit he saw wrong with Piper.

The drive is short and completely quiet. Shadow doesn't ask a word and I don't offer any information as I work to stay focused and inside my head so I can come face to face with the man responsible for what Piper went through.

"Open your eyes," I roar in anger as I kick in the right knee of this piece of shit prospect, shattering it with my steel toed boot. He screams in pain and yet I feel nothing but joy, sinister joy knowing that every second the pains burns through his beaten body.

"Who do you work for?" I don't give him a chance to answer before my right hand connects with the left side of his face and the sound of his teeth cracking fills the air.

"If you want to die, this is your chance to answer these questions. No one will find you here, I can keep you alive and torture you every fucking day if that's what it takes. My own personal form of hell just for you, so it's your decision." Again I strike with force to the same shattered knee. His screams echo again and I feed off of his pain like a fucking high I used to crave. Each time I hit him, I think about Piper and how they didn't give her any mercy as they tortured her. This only makes my job easier.

I pace in front of him, never taking my eyes away from his. "Did you rape her?" I decide to cut straight to the fucking chase with this shit. If he touched her like that, I'm cutting his fucking dick off.

"No." He's terrified for his life, but I can tell he's telling the truth about this.

"What did you do while they tortured her?" He doesn't respond, so I move in closer.

"What did you fucking do when they ruined her?" I kick his other knee, sending him into a screaming fit before he answers.

"Held the chain." This doesn't make me feel any better.

"You fucking took her to them, then held her in place so they could rape her. To me it's the same." I hear Blade turn on the blowtorch and actually look forward to him burning the fuck out of this guy. He fucking deserves to rot in hell and it may as well start right here.

"I'm giving you one last chance to talk before I burn your dick with a damn blowtorch. Who are you working for?" He cries out and doesn't even try to talk until Blade moves the torch toward his jeans.

"If I talk will you let me go quickly?" He wants to make a deal now that the fire is literally an inch from burning him.

"Talk and then I'll decide." Blade growls in his face and I watch the turmoil on this guy's face as he chooses to speak.

"Snipe." Blade takes a step back and I move forward.

"Why should we believe you?" His response has me even angrier than I was before. Something like this will be the death of the club as we know it. When Clutch talked about someone on the inside, I never dreamed it would be an officer that I consider a brother.

"Because I have no reason to lie. We all know I'm dead."

"You got that fucking right." Blade begins to walk and mumble as he does. I've seen him lose his shit before, but I've never felt the same level of rage as he's showing during one of these runs like I do tonight. I just want to end this guy, but I know we need to pull more information from him before I get to finish him off.

"Prove it!" Blade demands. "Fucking call him. Tell him you escaped and there was a struggle. That your weasley ass managed to kill us and now you need him here to clean up before you're caught."

Blade pulls the phone from Chewy's pocket and dials Snipe. "If you even hint that he's in danger coming here, I will personally remove each finger one by one then cauterize what's left so you don't bleed out. You'll feel everything and I'll enjoy the fuck out of making you suffer. Am I clear?"

There's no delay before Chewy answers. The phone rings and time seems to stand still as we wait impatiently.

"Who is this?" Snipe answers with a long pause.

"Boss it's me, I escaped but there was a struggle. Blade and Switch are dead; I know I fucked up, but it was either them or me. I need you here at the yard now, help me out before this gets any more fucked up!" Chewy cries out into the phone with frantic emotion that fits both the situation he's pretending to be in and the one he's met in reality. "Come around back. I have the front locked up and I'm on look out."

"I'll be there in two minutes, I'm right around the corner."

The phone goes dead and we wait for a few minutes before we hear the roar of Snipe's engine roll up. I signal for Blade to stay hidden, but he stands directly in the center of the room gun drawn, waiting for Snipe.

I better make the first move because if I don't, there's no telling what Blade is thinking or how he'll respond. I back myself against the wall and listen to the footsteps coming from outside. There's a pause almost as if the air is still and the whole world has stopped for this very moment. My heart is beating relentlessly because the thought of putting a bullet in my brother's head has my mind uneasy. I can tell when Snipe reaches for the door, the knob moves and Chewy lets out a loud yell at the same time.

Before Chewy has the time to finish yelling the word 'run', Blade has put a bullet in the back of his head and fired two shots through the door. There's a loud thump as Snipe's body hits the ground.

Fuck. Blade just killed him and now the last person that could possibly tell us anything is dead along with the only person to give us any clue as to who did this. Just then I hear Snipe scream in agony and before I have the time to blink, Blade is kicking the door open and has his pistol at Snipe's head and a knee in his chest.

"You didn't think I'd just gun you down now, did you Snipe? No, that'd be too easy. I made sure to drop you and now I have you at my will, which is much worse than hell will be now that I know you're a fucking traitor in my club." Blade's words flow from his mouth like poison gas fills the air, almost taking all the life from everything.

The hate and anger is so vivid I watch Snipe's face pale as he takes in every single word he growls out. "Now let's pull these bullets out and have some fun for old times sake, why don't we? Look, I even brought Switch to join the party." Blade pulls him up by the hair on his head to make him look at me then buries the barrel to the wound in his right shoulder as Snipe screams in agony. "This one in your leg should come out real nicely; looks like it might be in the bone. That'd be a shame to take your whole left leg so quickly but I can't have you dying on me, now can I? Switch get a saw; it looks like we're gonna have to amputate." Blade is in his insane state and I have to say this time I fucking welcome it. Anything he pulls out of that fucked up head of his is not going to be justice enough for what has happened.

Blade drags Snipe through the door to the shop and begins to order me around. "Call Beast. Tell him to stop looking for those fuckers and get to the hospital to watch over the girls. I don't know how fucking deep this shit runs and he's the only other solid I know for sure right now." I step to the back of the shop to make the call because Blade instantly begins to yell at Snipe.

"Where do you need me?" Beast answers, ready to go. I fill him in on his orders and end the call quickly. I need to hear how Snipe responds to Blade's interrogation because I have a few things I need to say to this mother fucker myself.

Chapter Eleven

Piper

I'm numb again. The shock of everything has consumed me entirely and I'm trying to grasp onto the shreds of reality that can keep me sane. The problem is, insanity is literally a moment away and I'm just not sure I can escape it this time.

The light from the single window in the room has had my attention for the last hour while we wait for my discharge papers. Any other day and I'd be raising hell to get out of here sooner, but today I feel safe in here. The confinements of this tiny room and the fact that there's only a single entrance that's being guarded makes me feel at ease.

"Looks like everything is set to go. Here are your follow up instructions and the scheduled times for your upcoming appointments." The nurse continues to talk and I watch in silence as Tori interacts with her. I look out the window and get lost in my head again.

"I'll make sure she gets all of this information down. Thank you so much for your help. Piper, your ride is here." Tori's voice pulls me from my thoughts and I look over to see a wheelchair waiting for me. She's holding the bag and my purse that she brought for me.

"I can walk." I quickly deny the ride, only to be told otherwise.

"It's protocol. I have to escort you to a vehicle in this chair. It's the only way out of here." The nurse laughs and I want to challenge her on that statement, but decide the battle isn't worth the effort. I give in and sit in the chair and wait to be pushed. When the door opens, I see Beast standing like he's ready to kill anyone who looks at us and I can't even offer him a teasing smile like I usually do. Sarge peers over at me with a sad expression and I quickly look down at my hands and ask Beast to go.

He begins to lead the way down the hall and we all follow in a line. It's like a damn parade until a female nurse tries to stop us for something. Tori and Sarge fall back to handle whatever is going on as I take a deep breath of fresh air the second we exit the doors.

Beast moves fast to get me into his truck and the second he closes the door I do what I know I have to do. "You remember that time you told me you'd do anything for me?" He nods as he climbs into the driver's seat.

"I need you to drive the fuck away right now and take me somewhere safe."

He grumbles as I practically beg. I can't go back to the club and the last thing I want to do is see how everyone looks at me now. "You're safe with me."

"No. I want to leave here and find a small town that I can go to until I can face everyone. Please don't make me watch what this does to everyone around me. At least you didn't look at me like I'm damaged." He looks forward as he starts the engine. It takes him a few seconds to put it in drive and actually pull away from the hospital, but he does it.

"Thank you." My words are soft and pathetic, but it's all I have in me right now. I know this will get him in deep shit with my brother and Switch, but I need to do this. I see him grab his phone and begin to text before we roll out of the parking lot completely. "Please text Sarge and make sure he stays with Tori."

"Already did." And with that he drives away.

He drives for hours without saying a word. It's the calm silence that I needed desperately. I watch the road pass for miles as I look out the window and try to make sense of what I'm going to do now. This is going to be tough on me, but I know I can't go back to the club. I have to decide where I want to move and try to start a new life away from all of the insanity that comes with being associated with all of that. My brother warned me about the dangers and I should've listened, but I didn't.

I hear him clear his throat, so I turn to look at him for the first time in a few hours. His dark hair is blowing from the window being cracked and his tattooed arms are bulging from his grip on the steering wheel. Beast reminds me so much of my brother and I think that's why I can relax with him. He's close enough to want to make sure I'm safe, but not close enough to be devastated about what happened. He doesn't ache just looking at me and that's something I need right now.

"You hungry?" His deep voice echoes throughout the truck and I just reply with a simple nod. There's not a chance in hell I could eat anything right now. My stomach is tied up in knots as I think about everything.

He stops for gas and I don't get out of the truck. The thought of moving isn't something I'm looking forward to. Glancing at the clock on the dash, I can tell we've been gone for over seven hours. *Seven.*

Just the thought of the number makes me nauseous all over again. Is it even possible that many men… "No. I can't do this." I kick open the door to get some fresh air while Beast finishes putting in the gas. My chest heaves as I try to act like I didn't just almost scream in hysterics because of a memory that is destined to haunt me for the rest of my life.

"You alright?" Beast steps up next to my open door when the sound of the nozzle clicks, showing the tank is full. He doesn't move to pull the hose from the truck, instead stepping closer to me.

"I'll be fine. Just give me a second." He watches me closely as I try to make the hot flash of hell pass. His patience is running out and I can feel it.

"I'm taking you to an old friend's house. She can help you through this shit and then I'm calling Blade and Switch."

"You can't." I immediately try to resist what he's saying only to be stopped.

"I have to tell them you're safe. After the shit that just went down, they'll be losing their minds when they find out you're not there anymore. I'm not sure if you've noticed, those two are fucking crazy when it comes to protecting what they love." Love. Even hearing him say it only makes me think he's just saying what he thinks I want to hear. I choose to ignore the 'L' word and try to get more information about where he plans to take me. It might just be time I make a clean break from anything to do with the club, and that may mean I have to somehow lose Beast on this journey. The sun's reflection off the hood of the truck catches my eye and I zone in on the light while I contemplate my response. There's no doubt that he'll be watching me closely. It'll take some creative maneuvering to get away from him and it's not like I'm prepared to go off on my own at this point. I need to think.

"Give me til' tonight. Then I'll call them myself." He nods and it seems he doesn't see through my intentions, but if he's anything like my brother, he'll pick up on it as we drive. I guess the fact that I'm still going through my own internal hell will help deflect anything he may pick up on.

I slide back against the seat of the truck and take in the pain across my back. I'm flooded with a memory of them cutting my back and it just dawns on me that I haven't looked at how bad the cuts are. I suddenly have the overwhelming desire to shower and scrub my skin clean again. "How far is your friend from here?"

He slides in again and starts the engine before he responds. "About an hour."

An hour feels like eternity as I fight the chaos in my mind. I want to cry and scream until I can't move from the exhaustion of releasing all of this. *The feel of the chains. The feel of their rough hands. The smell of their breath. The burn as the knife cuts my skin…* "Stop the truck!" I scream at Beast as I reach for the handle. We aren't at a complete stop when I throw the door open and throw up all down the seat of his truck.

The second we aren't moving, I take off running. It's an open field of knee high weeds and nothing else in close vicinity.

I start off frantic and then become focused on a single tree in the distance. It gets further away as I run, but I try like hell to get to it. It's just too far. I run until I collapse.

I lie in the weeds and look up into a bright blue sky. I'm not even sure how far I travelled, but for a few minutes I didn't feel the pain all over my body. I didn't feel the ache inside my chest and deep within my soul. I was simply running from the everything in the world with no purpose or plan. And for one second that felt fucking amazing.

Chapter Twelve

Switch

We've beaten Snipe bloody at this point; the stench of dry blood and burnt skin fills the air. Every time he tries to pass out, Blade shoots him up with the crank he took out of Snipe's bag. Apparently he'd been using for a while from the looks of what he was carrying. Snipe never really showed signs of abuse or Blade would've kept his ass in check. He can tolerate pretty much everything with the exceptions of drugs and lying.

"Snipe, you little drug addicted bastard. How many fucking times have I pulled your ass out of this shit in the past? You told me this shit was over!" Blade roars out as he continues to beat Snipe unmercifully like a he's a human punching bag. "I gave you so many chances, I let you wallow in your own self-pity, I took care of you every time you came off a bender, and for what? For you to fall back into this shit years later and betray me and my fucking club?"

Blade's words hold so much disgust it only fuels my anger more, as if everything between us was in sync. I grab Snipe by the hair and hold his head up to look Blade in the eyes. I want him to see everything I see. Speaking through the lump in my throat, I growl my words into his ear. "You knew this would happen. You helped destroy the only thing I've ever loved and now she doesn't even want to look at me." I feel more anger rising from the words leaving my mouth. A new wave of hurt flows through me, almost as if me saying it aloud makes it more real. "But here, right here. I am judge, jury, and executioner. Here I am the giver of life and distributor of death and you," I pause only to subdue the rage for a moment, "will suffer worse than you could ever imagine." I grip tight onto Snipe's hair as I strike his face again and again, feeling the destruction with every blow.

"That's enough!" Blade grips tightly onto my shoulder. "We still need him to talk." This time he wants to let the fucker talk. Blade is fucking bipolar with this shit and yet again I disagree with how he wants to handle this. It's just the first time I'm on the more destructive side of the fence.

"It's Jynx MC."

"What?" I barely hear Snipe speak through the moaning that comes out of his mouth.

"Jynx, they promised me the club when they ran you off. I owed them. The crank; my debt would have been my life. I gave them insight on the club, told them who we were dealing guns to, and told them whatever they wanted to know. They promised they weren't going to harm any of you. Just that they wanted the information, so they knew who had stock with us. I knew they were getting their guns from the cartel so I didn't think they were trying to deal. I promise, I never meant for any of this to happen."

"That's a fucking lie and you know it. You piece of shit. When that prospect called you and said boss, you knew exactly what he was talking about." I dig my thumb into the open wound on his shoulder. "Tell me the fucking truth or I'm taking one of your eyes next." I'm overcome with rage as I place my thumb against his eye. "Tell me right fucking now before I dig it out."

"What do you want? For me to tell you I wanted you all gone so I could have the club to myself?" Snipe laughs and spits blood at my boots. "There's nothing you can do to stop him now. He has everything he needs to end you both or land you in jail. That shit with Clutch that went down, if you think that wasn't all a part of this, you're fucking crazy. That was nothing." He continues to laugh to himself before Blade's fist connects with his stomach and leaves him gasping for air.

"Then who the fuck was it? Otherwise this torture will continue to drag on," Blade says with the taste of blood already in his mouth, hungry like a shark that's already taken the first bite of its victim.

"Why don't you ask him yourself?" Snipe grins as if he has a chance in hell of surviving this. "You think he isn't on his way here with me missing?"

"I think he's not concerned with you being gone one bit; if you're out of the picture he has everything for himself. At least if it were me I wouldn't give a shit about some piece of shit like you." Blade's words seem to make reality hit Snipe right in the chest; his face turns sour as he spews the next few words.

"At least this club won't belong to an outsider." Blade stands back and widens his stance. It's as if he's trying to stay sturdy on his feet while he takes in everything he's saying.

"So, it's been him all along? Tex's bastard son, huh? Let me guess. Devils of Eden promised your own MC under their protection and all the crank your petty heart desires right?"

"Fuck you! You think you could just take the club after everything Tex did for us? Yeah, he thought of you as his son and always praised you over all of us. You were the fucking golden boy; always fucking perfect in his eyes. Switch, Beast, Sarge… everyone thought you were some kind of god. You're not. You're just another fucking loser like the rest of them and then you began ruining everything that was perfect."

The fury that's rumbling deep inside me can't be contained. Piper was ruined because of the petty bullshit that mother fucker believes. This was never going to be his club. Tex removed him from it for a reason and it never even occurred to me that after Tex's death, James would try to get it back. My mind snaps and the world goes black. All I can feel is the burn on my fists as I continue to smash the remnants of what was once Snipe's face.

My own heavy breathing is all I hear when I stop to look at him as the warm blood splatters on my face. The world is cold and I have only one thought as I begin to come back to reality. *James will die tonight.*

"Switch let it go. We need to get the guys. It's time to find James." Blade's voice echoes for a moment until I snap back to reality.

"Tell them to meet us at the clubhouse we need to roll in loaded, wipe every one of those fuckers off the map." My eyes glance over the room as I look for anything giving evidence that I was the one who ended his life. Without any other reason to stay, I turn to continue this rage.

"Agreed, I already sent out the text. Let's ride."

We ride fast to the club; the wind seems to bring my senses back to life, making me crave destroying these fuckers more by the second. When we arrive at the club, everyone is already inside. We both rush in with more determination than we've ever had. They fucked up when they touched Piper.

"Grab every weapon you can get your hands on. Snipe is gone. All of this shit is on him and I'm ending this tonight." Silence falls over the officers. I get it. They've lost someone they thought was a brother, but the hate fueling my body at the moment doesn't give a shit about him for letting all this happen to everyone. To the one woman I… I can't think that way right now. I can't let anything into my mind that will weaken me. Every single Devil will die tonight by our hands, whether they were responsible or not. I refuse to leave a loose end that can come back to haunt me after this night.

Sarge throws the door open and Tori follows him through it. My heart sinks as I wait for Piper to follow even though the last thing I want her to do is be around anyone in this club until we get to the bottom of everything.

"Where's Beast?" I yell out in frustration when he doesn't walk in either.

"He's with Piper, they left town. I just got off the phone with him," Blade says as he walks around the corner tossing me a semi-automatic rifle. "I'm having Sarge take Tori to meet them and they can both keep the girls safe until we can clean this up."

"What the fuck?" I scream in frustration as I kick the coffee table across the room. She left town without a call? "When did she get out of the hospital?" I have a shit ton of questions and no damn answers. I swear this night only gets worse as the minutes pass.

Why in the fuck did this happen to Piper? Why did they think they could use her to take over the club? They had to know we'd lose our shit with what they did. You'd think they'd come in under the radar to get shit done, but no these fuckers aren't the slightest sane.

I want to stop and talk to Tori as I walk outside, but I don't. I'd love more than anything to ask about Piper and for Tori to tell me that she's completely healed and everything will go back to normal right after this run, but I know it won't.

It'll never be like it was before, when for once I felt like I had actually found someone.

Chapter Thirteen

Piper

"You fuckin' done running?" Beast walks up slowly and continues to look at the horizon as he talks to me and smokes a cigarette. "You do realize that I'm not going to run your ass down. If you want to stay safe, you keep your sassy fucking ass with me." He paces back and forth at my feet. "I know this is all fucked up and you've been through a lot, but don't make me regret getting you out of there to get yourself together." I roll my eyes and stare into the sky even longer. He has no idea what I've been through.

"You know what I've been through? You know what it feels like? I don't know if I had one or seven men rape me. Seven. Do you fucking hear me? Seven." I sit up as hatred begins to boil in my throat as I scream the number over and over.

"I went black. My mind shut off to protect me and now all I'm doing is wondering what really happened." He looks down at me when a tear falls down my cheek. He sits beside me in the only awkward way a giant tattooed man would and remains quiet while he waits for me to continue.

"How am I supposed to get past this?" My words are barely a whisper as I try like hell to talk over the lump in my throat.

"I'm not sure. But I know you're the strongest woman I know and you have one hell of a club behind you." He moves the dirt below his hand and watches over the horizon, protecting me the entire time.

"I can't go back there. It's because of the club that this happened." I stop talking as a flash of memory rushes over me. The way he wanted to talk to Blade confirms that. Fucking hell. Just knowing they all heard what they did is enough reason to never show my face again.

"If you think you have a choice, you're more insane that I thought. You're tied to the club and there's a few of us that won't rest without you being taken care of." I want to remind him I was at the club when I was kidnapped and that it was the club yard that I was tortured in, but I don't. There's no reason to blame this on the club. I went against everything my brother tried to get me to do. He didn't want me near the club, but I demanded it.

I wanted him back in my life knowing it would be a tough adjustment, I just never dreamed how bad it could be. And I sure as hell didn't expect to fall for one of his guys as hard as I did Switch, but that doesn't matter anymore. There's no way I could ever go back to the club now that this has all happened.

"I've lived most of my life on my own, I'll be fine." He exhales loudly when I show rebellion to his suggestion.

"You're coming with me to an old friend's house. She'll be able to keep you safe. Under no circumstances do you ever share where I'm taking you with anyone. This is her safe house and I've worked hard to make sure it's the best there is. The fact that I'm taking you there should tell you how much I care about your stubborn ass." He stands up and holds his hand out to help me up and I just look at him as I take in the fresh air around me one more time.

If it was only feasible for me to stay in this field and feel the peace I'm going through right now, I'd never leave. But I know it's not and no matter how much I don't want to find a new home, that's what I have to do.

Taking his hand, I let him guide me to my feet. Our slow walk back to the truck is silent and I wonder what he's thinking while I reflect on the sadness in my heart as I leave behind a part of myself.

He opens the truck door and I step inside and slide into the seat, trying to ignore the pain from moving like that. He looks away as my face fails to hide it and I appreciate him for not making a scene about it. The only way to forget about all of this is to do everything I can to not let what happened define me.

"You alright?" He waits until he's behind the wheel to ask.

"Never better," I say with a smile and he sends me a smirk in return before he begins to drive us down the road again.

Switch

We all meet at the north warehouse to plot our next move. It's killing me to make plans when I want to obliterate their clubhouse and anyone who gets in my way.

"I need eyes inside before we do some stupid shit." Blade takes this moment to actually think strategically and not lead a free for all of mass murders like I want to. I should feel comfort in that, but it irritates me.

"No. I don't need fucking eyes. I have my own. Follow me in or I'll handle this shit myself." I kick my leg to start my bike and drive fast until I'm headed straight for their club. It isn't long before I've driven through the fucking front door of the Devil's MC and end up in a slide on my side as I sweep a few of these fuckers off their feet. I can hear engines follow in behind me and guns firing before we've taken over the house and have every guy here on their knees and scared out of their fucking minds.

"What the fuck." One of their patched leaders speaks up as he struggles with the grip Tank has on his neck as he's slammed into the wall a few times.

"Where's James?" Not a single mother fucker makes a sound. Rage continues to be my fuel as I pace in front of each of them trying to decide who to kill first.

Piper flashes through my mind and the way she looked when I found her in the salvage yard and I'm gutted all over again.

At least one of the fuckers in front of me had something to do with her attack and it takes everything inside me not to open fire on each of them individually right now with no questions asked. I don't need their lies to know they've done something to deserve death today. It's how this club is run. I wouldn't expect anything different from anything James had a part of.

"Where the fuck is James?" I scream like a lunatic and pull the one with the balls to question us to his feet.

"Must be fucking your girl." The instant he speaks, I lose my shit. No punch to his face is hard enough. Not a single thing could stop me from killing him as I pound his head against the wall until he's no longer breathing. My grip on his neck is only released as I catch another one of their officers watching me. Dropping the dead weight to the ground, I look around the room and move to the young one with the guilty look on his face.

"Where in the fuck is James?" He starts to stutter and I stick a pistol in his mouth and move very close to his face. Sweat drops from my forehead onto his nose and I repeat myself very slowly. "Where is James? You get one fucking chance to answer me."

"He skipped town."

"Chicken shit motherfucker!" Tank yells out just as he responds and before I have a chance to say anything else, Blade is standing side by side with me.

"Did you have anything to do with that girl at the salvage yard the other day?" His breathing quickly increases and panic fills his eyes. I grip his hair and hold his head back so I can look into this fucker's eyes.

"They made me hold the chains. I swear I didn't touch her."

"You fucking held her while they raped her." My voice is filled with rage as I spit my words in his face. My hold on his hair gives me enough leverage to throw him on his back and stand over him with my gun over his skull.

"If you want to take another breath, tell me who was there that night." He shakes his head no to me as tears run down his face.

"I'm dead either way." He knows the deal. We all know what's going to happen. It's the way of the club. Revenge has to be taken and they all knew it would be when they kidnapped her.

"But will they find your family and take it out on the ones you love like I will?" Blade steps forward with a murderous look in his eyes that tells this fool below us that he will do anything to find the information we're asking for.

"Don't you say one fucking word, Ray. You shut your goddamned mouth." One of the idiots on the ground begins spewing his bullshit before Tank points his gun and shoots him in the head. I never take my eyes off of Ray below me and just squat down beside him. He needs to understand just how serious I am.

"Was he one of them?" He shakes his head no to me. I mentally begin counting. *Seven.* James is one of them, I know. Our prospect and Ray must've held the chains. So that leaves four more that I need to identify before I blow this fucking place up for the simple reason that they call this their house.

"Who else was there that night?" I hold the gun closer to his face and his eyes move to the guy I just beat to death.

"That fucker was one of them? Did he rape her?" I feel my entire body tense up as I wait for his answer and when he takes too long, I decide to grab him by his scrawny ass neck and lift him to his feet before I smash him into the wall. He's trembling as my grip tightens and his breathing is constrained simply because I want it to be. His life is literally in my hands… and he knows it.

"How many raped her?" I don't even recognize my own voice at this point.

"Two because you showed up." Rage flows through me as the guilt swells up just knowing that if I had been a few minutes earlier, everything she went through could've been prevented.

"And you just watched and waited for your turn." My fingers grip his neck tighter as I watch the life slowly pull away from his face. He will die today by my hands, but I need more information before that happens, so I release just enough to let him breathe. "Who else?"

He looks into my eyes and shakes his head no to me before he speaks around the tightness of my grip on his neck. "You'll kill me anyway. I'm already a fucking rat. I'll let it fester within the depths of your soul while you try to figure out the others." And with that my fingers tighten. My insides twist until a guttural roar escapes me and I work to kill another man with my bare hands.

I have zero remorse as he scrapes my arm, grasping for his last breath. He watches my eyes until I let loose once again. I look around the room at the filth still breathing even though we're holding them all at gunpoint on their knees. Not a single one of them look at me as I scour the room for any sign of information. "There's three more, start asking questions until we get some fucking answers. Find someone that means something to this fucker I'm holding." I turn to look him in the eyes once again, making sure he hears me loud and clear. "Bring in his kid if that's what it takes."

Piper

The sound of Beast's voice wakes me and I find myself curled up in the seat of his truck. The window is down, but the sun is still beating through the windshield, making me hot and sticky. "You gonna sleep all day?" I can tell he's leaning over me, so I throw an arm over my forehead to try to ignore him.

"Nice try, stubborn ass. Don't make me carry you." He teases me as he opens the truck door and the sound of a female voice startles me and has me sitting up quickly to see where we are. I stop moving as my eyes begin to take it all in. Everything is gorgeous and calm. Trees surround us with the exception of a large cabin to my right. I glance over Beast's shoulder to see the girl behind the voice and see nothing but beauty in her face.

How in the hell does he know someone who looks so… normal? She looks like your innocent girl next door and I can't even fathom how in the hell she could be one of his ex-girlfriends. "Please come inside. I'll show you to your room and you can get some real rest." Even her voice is calm. She seems nice and all put together. Her clothes and heels make me jealous as I follow her inside. I look like a homeless person with my baggy t-shirt and sweatpants, but honestly I haven't cared what I look like.

I take in the large living room and kitchen as we walk through the main part of the house. Everything is in its place and even though I try to catch the pictures on the mantle, I miss them while we walk past.

"Here's the bathroom. Towels are in here." She opens a closet full of brand new items and starts to pull a few soaps and lotions out. "I picked up some things I thought you might need. I'm sure I forgot something, so please just let me know what else you need and I'll get it for you." She sets the stuff in my hands then continues to walk down the hallway until she enters the last door on the right.

"Here's your bedroom. It's yours for as long as you need it." She opens the closet to show me a few dresses and t-shirts and even points to a robe at the back of the closet. "I know it's just the basics and I promise I'll help you get it all as soon as you feel up to it. But for now, it'll get you by so you can rest." I look down as she walks past. I know I need to say thank you because I truly do appreciate everything, but the reality of it is, I don't want to need someone to get me things. That's not who I am. "Thank you." I force the words from my mouth as she steps into the doorway.

"You're welcome." Our eyes meet for a brief second before I look down again. I don't want her knowing how broken I am.

"You know you can run, but you can't hide from these guys. When they love you they'll tear up the world to find you."

"Who's to say one of them loves me?" I respond, trying to divert her from speaking what I already know.

"I can see the hurt on your face and I can tell by the way Beast is protecting you. There's nothing like leaving the club to run from the hurt. I've been there. Hell, I live with it every day." She starts to close the door before I ask the most important question.

"Does it get any easier?"

"No. But you learn to deal with it. You'll eventually decide that the time you had was worth the ache you live with, but it still hurts like hell every damn day." I watch her pull the door closed and take in the complete silence. The room is nice, but it's not my home. I can use it to get on my feet, but I'll have to move on very soon if I want to make a clean break from everyone.

There's a long mirror in the corner and I avoid it as I walk through the room. The last thing I want to see is how I look. I can feel how I look and it's disgusting. Why would I want to go back to being repulsed as I see the bruises and marks all over again?

There's a stereo on the dresser and out of curiosity, I hit the power button hoping to hear something good come through the speakers. An old country song begins to play and I'm relieved. It's safe for me to listen to and not have a reminder of what I'm running from. The slow tempo makes the perfect background noise for me to sleep. If I'm lucky, I'll sleep for a few days and this will all be over once I wake up.

I lie on the bed and cover up with the small blue blanket that was draped over the headboard. I don't let myself think about anything. The numbness has silenced all of my thoughts and it's the safest place for me to be right now.

It's a matter of minutes before I can feel myself giving in to sleep once again and I don't fight it.

Chapter Fourteen

Switch

Blade forces me out of the room the second I mention bringing in a kid to see this. It's something I never intended to do, but if that's what it takes to get the answers I need to avenge Piper's attack, then that's what I'll fucking do. The kid will never be hurt, but I won't let Ray know that.

"Get your shit together Switch. I'm not bringing a kid in to see this massacre. We need to get this done and get the fuck out of here." His boots sound heavy as he paces in front of me. He calls the shots in the club and every other time I've obeyed and backed him even if I had to say my peace afterward, but not this time. This is my run and I'm not going to end this until I find out who else had a part in ruining Piper.

"Not a fucking chance, Blade. I have to do this for her. She deserves to know that she's safe from the men who attacked her and if it takes me 'til my dying day, I'll find them all." I wipe the sweat from my forehead and watch him as he hears me yet again stand up to him about a run.

"Did I fucking miss where you took the head of the table? Because lately you seem to think you call the mother fucking shots."

"No, but on this one, I have to get the answers and I'm confused as fuck that you're not backing me on this. She's your sister, for fuck's sake." He stops moving and glares at me over his shoulder. I can feel his anger, but today it doesn't affect me. It's nothing compared to the hate I'm feeling inside knowing that the men who did this to her still have a breath in their body.

"I fucking know who she is. But I also can't risk my entire club while you torture revenge each one who may have had something to do with her. We end it now and we can finish shit later. The entire club will go before I'm done with this so we will get all of them."

He slams his fist into the wall before he runs his hands through his hair like he's trying to get a grip and I want nothing more than to go back in that room and light every one of those fuckers on fire.

I push off the wall and slam the door open to see that Tank and the prospects have all the guys against the wall with the exception of Ray. My eyes make contact with the man that will be providing me the information I need to end this manhunt one way or another. I reach down and lift him up by his hair and begin to drag him over the men against the wall. Forcing him to stand and face them is a pain in the ass, but I need him to talk.

"Which one of these fuckers touched her?" I look to any of them for a reaction, only to be denied any sign either way. When he doesn't respond right away, I swallow hard and order the one command I may one-day regret. "Go find the kid and I'll call you with the location to meet me." The prospect moves quickly, probably wanting out of this fucking mess before it gets any worse. Ray begins to cry out knowing I'm pulling in the leverage to make him talk.

There's four on the wall. I need three men identified. I want more than anything for all of them to be in here, but something tells me it won't be that easy. Tank yanks one of them to his feet and holds him in front of us while I force Ray to answer me. "Was this fucker there?" He nods his head yes and without another thought, I end the fucker's life with a bullet. I move us a few feet further until we're in front of an older man. My stomach hurls at the thought of him even seeing her naked. Ray actually speaks this time. "Not him. He's innocent." I aim my gun at the old man's head and think about how to proceed. Looking down, I catch a glimpse of the cross on his neck and reach to get a better look. I recognize it from somewhere, but I can't seem to place it.

"Please don't. He's my father. He was here to get me to leave the club when you stormed through the door. He's never done anything wrong in his life except love me more than I deserve." Blade stands next to us now and I catch a look on his face that tells me we aren't going to agree on the old man, but that's not something I want to deal with right now.

"If you want him to live, tell me who the last two are." I no longer recognize my own voice or the raging thoughts that have taken over my head.

"The last two are right there."

"Fucking liar!" the guy on the end screams out the second Ray seals his death sentence. I don't have to take care of the last two, Blade was more than eager to handle them before I had to even say anything. I shove my gun in the old man's back and move Ray next to him as I lead them both to the door. "Clean this shit up. Wipe this club out. I'm taking the truck. Someone get my bike." Shoving them both through the door I leave knowing this club has seen its last day. Tank knows what to do and my only focus is finding James right now. Ray seems to be the only one willing to talk… even if it's forced. I have his father and I'll have his kid soon. If he knows anything, he'll talk.

"Where's James?" I ask him one last time. He knows it's his last chance, but only closes his eyes and shakes his head no to me.

"I don't know."

"Get the fuck in the truck." One last shove to Ray sends him into the side of the truck and him losing his footing. I don't shove his father and try to process exactly what I'm going to do with this guy. He has to know his son is about to die.

"Put this over your eyes and get on the floor." I toss a shirt at the old man, yank open the back door, and stand impatiently as I wait for him to crawl in. He moves slowly and the way he moves reminds me of my grandfather from the back. That pisses me off even further so I take it out on Ray before I shove him into the front seat.

"Sit your ass in that seat and don't move a fucking muscle." I hear Blade at my back before I can close the door and lock Ray in.

"I'm coming with you." Blade speaks sternly as he mounts his bike and lights up a cigarette. He wants me to argue, but I won't. I don't give a fuck if he comes with me, it won't change the way it turns out.

"Meet me at the salvage yard." I text TJ and tell him to bring the kid to the yard as well. The smell of gasoline draws my attention to the jugs in the back and it's in this moment that I take a deep breath and enjoy the smell. I know this will obliterate all but one of the maggots that had Piper.

Just as I lift two of the jugs out, Tank meets me at the tailgate. "I'll meet you back at the house as soon as I'm done here."

"I'll be there when I'm done. We have to find James." He nods as he takes the jugs and walks back inside. Blade takes off down the road before I have the chance to sit in the driver's seat. Glancing over to Ray, I see a man wearing regret all over his soul. It's too bad he didn't have the guts to do something about his club holding a woman seven to one.

"I'm sorry I didn't stop them." His whisper echoes through the cab right before I start the engine.

"Me too."

Chapter Fifteen

Switch

The dried blood on the chain makes me irate when I pick it up. I know it's hers. It hasn't been near long enough for it to be washed away. I swallow hard and let it remind me of the reason I'm here. I'll let it fuel me and get the revenge Piper deserves.

It's took almost a day to find Ray's son, but we finally managed it. It's the leverage I know I need to get the answers from him if he has any. We've all tortured him and tried to make him talk, but he's not budging with the traditional methods I promised Blade I'd try first. I held up my end of the bargain and now it's time to do shit my way.

I slide my hair out of my face just as I move closer to Ray. He's trembling, but still seems to have this cocky fucking demeanor about him that tells me not to fall for his shit. I go in loud and demanding. He gets one more opportunity to make me not rip his skin from his body piece by piece while he stays coherent for all of it.

"Tell me everything you know about James. Where would he go? My guys are flipping shit upside down until we find him." The chain hangs heavy in my hand as I wait for a response from him. My mind is swirling with an image of Piper from that night. Her lifeless body hanging from the very chain I hold in my hands and her dried tears and blood painted all over her body continue to haunt me as I pace. This fucker literally held her tight so other men could rape her. He may as well have stuck his own dick in her as far as I'm concerned because I can't allow him to live.

I stop pacing and stand in front of him, looking into his eyes for one ounce of sincerity when and if he decides to talk. His father stands beside him and Blade moves in beside me. TJ has Ray's son on standby if Ray chooses not to take me seriously, but I hope to hell that's a card I never have to play.

"James never talked about where he was going. Some of the guys thought he'd go on the road because he knew you'd be looking for blood." I walk slowly again and let the chain drag on the ground behind me. Blade stands with his arms crossed and glares at Ray. In a way I'm surprised he hasn't snapped and ripped his fucking heart out just because he's tired of waiting. That's how Blade would be normally.

"Where on the road?" I pass in front of him once more, not letting my eyes leave his.

"They never told me. I swear on everything I'd tell you if I knew." I don't know whether to believe him or call him out for thinking I'm stupid, but what I'm getting from him isn't guilt or an apologetic plea. He's far too comfortable with the way this has all gone down. Maybe he thinks because he has ratted out all of his brothers that I won't now ruin him as well. *It's too bad he's a stupid mother fucker.*

Another memory of Piper flashes in my mind. This time was from when she was in the hospital. She was so goddamn broken and I couldn't fucking fix her. She needed me and the only thing I could do was leave her to find the men who did this to her. Something tells me she's already working on her goodbye to me if I ever get the chance to see her again.

The thought of that makes me fucking snap.

I throw the chain around his neck and wrap it tight while I watch Ray start to struggle for air. The desperation in his eyes shows how much he wants to, but of course he can't move with his hands bound behind his back. Tossing the chain over the ballast above his head, I pull the slack out until he begins to lift off the ground. He struggles as he coughs blood and fights for air at the same time and the sound of him fighting brings a sense of composure to my mind. He deserves to die by this chain. I see the look on Ray's father's face and don't feel an ounce of guilt. He knows the end is coming for his son, what he doesn't know is just how bad the torture can be and exactly what I'm capable of now that they've found my weak spot.

"Last chance Ray, don't make this any more painful than it's already going to be. Tell me where James is before I make you watch both your father and your son die."

"Fuck you, I told you there's nothing to tell you." Before the words finish leaving Ray's mouth, I trigger my switch blade and stab his father right in the throat. Blood floods from the wound as I pull the knife and look at Ray as his father gasps for air. The blood fills his lungs quickly and the sound of death is imminent as he reaches for his son.

"His death was quick compared to what I'll make yours if you don't cooperate. Now the only choices you have to make is how fast you die and whether or not you watch your son die before you do." He's still losing his shit over seeing his father die, which is understandable, but the shift in his eyes tells me he's finally getting the picture of what I'm willing to do to avenge what happened to Piper.

"Fuck you! You don't even know where he is." He gives one last pathetic attempt at pretending he has the upper hand, but we all know who'll have the last say in all of this.

"Blade, dial TJ. Let's give him his fuckin' proof." Blade barely shifts to pull his phone out of his pocket; his raging demeanor is still very much fueling my own. He's just taking the quiet role this time, knowing this is something I need to handle even though he's just as fucking irate. TJ answers quickly and Blade makes sure it's loud enough to hear everything on speaker.

TJ makes some noise and then we hear a young voice that for the first time since Piper's attack makes me feel slight regret. "I wanna go home."

"That's enough, take him home, just promise me you won't hurt him." The words almost infuriate me as he spews them from his pathetic mouth. The look I shoot back at him tells him enough to continue. I'm not sure why he thinks I should show him any loyalty when he literally held Piper in place for James and these fucking assholes to fuck her.

"He knows where she is, hopefully I held you fuckers back long enough. You can kill me, kill us all but I'd rather be dead than suffer in your world."

I yank hard on the chain, pulling Ray's feet from the ground. He kicks back and forth as his body convulses trying to free itself from the chain crushing its windpipe. The tears roll from his eyes and the sounds of his struggle come to an abrupt end.

"Call Beast right fucking now Blade, we need to go. Fuck all of this! I'm headed to the safe house now! Goddamnit, he knows where she is. Why was I so fucking stupid to trust anyone to keep her safe? I'm done with this shit and if she's not safe I'm walking away from this fucking club to make sure she's never in danger again." He stares at me as he waits for an answer.

"There's no fucking service. I'm sending a text to everyone to get back to the clubhouse, we're going now." We sprint for the bikes. My gut is killing me and I hope like fuck Beast is there to take this fucker down before he even gets close to her or I'll kill him too. There's nothing I wouldn't do now to save her and make her life normal again. *I can only hope I make it in time.*

Piper

The house is silent and the only sound I hear is the creaking of the wood floor as I tiptoe down the hall. It seems as though I'm here by myself, but I can't imagine Beast leaving me here like that. It's weird being in a strange and quiet house after being at the club around all the guys for months. I miss their crazy more than I thought

I would. I think I slept for two days straight and only woke up when that woman brought food in.

I walk the halls and look at the pictures of all the people I don't recognize, wondering how Beast knows this woman. She's been so nice to me even though she has no idea who I am. Could she really see how broken I was and she's just showing me pity? I guess it doesn't matter why she's helped me, having a safe place to sleep is worth whatever guilty feelings I'll make myself feel the next few days.

"What's her name?" I whisper out loud to myself, curiosity finally taking over and flooding my brain. It's nice to be able to think about something other than my own nightmares, even if it ends up being short lived. It's never long and I'm tortured with another constant reminder of what I've been through the last couple days.

She seems so happy in all these pictures, maybe she was right about it getting better. Maybe there is hope for me. My walk down the long hall leads me to the kitchen and my eyes land on a coffee pot immediately. The taste of some good coffee becomes my only focus and I smile when I see everything out and ready for me to make a pot. *She really is like some perfect house wife isn't she?*

The smell invades my senses and for a split second makes me feel like I will actually be able to move forward.

It may be a slow one step at a time process, but I'll make it. When the coffee finishes brewing, I pour a giant cup and make my way back to my room. If the smell of coffee makes me feel like this, a shower will have me feeling like a completely new woman and that's something I think I need desperately.

A glimpse in the mirror solidifies just how bad I thought I looked. Holy shit I look fucking terrible and there's no way a shower and a cup of coffee will fix this mess, but at least it's a start. While the water is heating up, I start to pull some of the makeup and soaps from the closet she showed me. I have to shake my head at just how thorough she was when she went shopping for me. It makes me feel bad because I know I would've forgotten half this shit if Switch had called me on the fly like that and told me to get everything a woman would need. I hope to never need this information, but I do take a mental note of everything she stocked.

The shower feels amazing. I adjust the water so that it's literally raining down on me and covering my body all at once. She bought me five scented soaps and I used every single one of them, inhaling each of them as they filled the air. The warmth wraps me up and for a little while I feel clean again. That's something I haven't felt in days.

I take my time getting dressed and even choose the brighter of the tank tops that's folded in the bedroom closet. Actually running a brush through my hair still hurts, but it's getting easier.

Once I feel more like a complete person than I've felt in days, I decide to look for Beast. Maybe I can get him to take me to get a few things before he inevitably heads back to the club. Plus, we need to sit down and have a real solid talk because he needs to know I won't be going back with him. Something tells me that will be a true struggle to manage, but I'm known for standing my ground when I'm determined.

I walk quietly through the open house, never seeing a sign of either Beast or the girl. There's one closed door, but I don't try to open it. I'm sure they'll hear me moving around and be out here soon enough. Maybe Beast likes this girl and he's getting some pussy. Lord knows his cranky ass needs to lighten up a little.

There's a large window at the back of the house where I can see a large deck. Stepping outside and getting the first bit of fresh air that I've had for days feels great. I look around for a chair with a perfect view and sit in peace while I finish my now cold coffee. This is absolute serenity. I could easily live here, it's just too bad it's associated with the club and Switch so that won't be an option.

I decide it's a great thing that I haven't run into either of them and move to top off my coffee and really get some quality time back on the deck before I end up facing the girl and Beast. Sliding the glass door closed I look to the front of the house quickly because I can still feel a breeze from outside coming from that direction. They must be bringing things in or something. Making my way back down the hall, I can hear the door close and it's not until I step into the dining room that I stop frozen in my footsteps.

It's him. I'll never forget that face. His hair. Those eyes. The nightmare that's haunted me since I first laid eyes on him. At first I can't tell if this is real or if I'm seeing things. *How could he be here? How could he have found me?*

Reality slaps me in the face as soon as he charges towards me. It takes me a split second to comprehend that this is all happening, but I manage to sprint for the kitchen. He somehow catches me and throws me head first into the cabinet. I can feel the wound on my forehead split open again and the warm blood begins to run down my face. He yanks me by the hair until I'm facing him. "Thought you could hide from me, did you?"

His words scorch my insides as I take in the reality that I'll never truly be safe again. He lifts me to my feet by pulling on my hair. My head is throbbing and I can hardly hear over the chaos floating through my mind. I'm terrified, but I'm mad as fuck. He can't have this much control of me. No one controls me.

"You little bitch, you thought you could come here and hide while this all blows over? I'll haunt you every day of your pathetic whore life." He grips between my legs, squeezing hard and making me gasp in pain. "This is my pussy. I'll take it whenever I goddamn please and there's not a damn thing you can do to stop me." What happened to me? Why do I feel completely vulnerable? Where is the woman who would've fought this piece of shit and tried to kill him where he stands?

Dig Piper. Fucking dig deep and find that badass bitch that doesn't bow down to anyone. If you can't dig for that girl, you may as well have died in that salvage yard.

Chapter Sixteen

Piper

I'm staring my nightmare in the face and my mind is battling the urge to go to my safe zone or stay coherent and fight this fucker this time. There's only one of him this time. He made the mistake of not drugging me and tying me up before he had his hands on me.

Oh god. The familiar stench of his foul breath has me gagging on my own vomit as the memories flood back to me. It's a mind fuck that's trying to cripple me, but I'm fighting so hard to stay sane.

I grit my teeth and force myself to focus because it's really the only choice I have to save myself. My back is against the broken cabinets and I feel myself start to slide lower as his grip on my hair shifts. "Let me just remind you again exactly who the fuck I am! You think your big brother and his punk friends can do anything to stop me? Remember who has control here. This is my world and you're just living in it because I'm allowing you to. If I want this pussy, it's mine. If I want the all of the Angels of Death dead, then it's done. If I want Blade's head on a silver fucking platter, it'll be delivered to me."

He starts to unbuckle his belt and my only thought is that I'll never escape him if I let him do this to me again. He will live to torture me in every way possible and the thought of him getting to Blade or Switch drives me into an entire new level of hatred for this filth. *This can't be how this goes. This can't be my story.* The sad shell of who I used to be won't be broken down by some vile piece of shit.

The click of gun silences the room while my frantic eyes find Beast in the doorway holding one at this guy's head. The air sits heavy and Beast's presence somehow gives me the added strength I need to face this nightmare head on. Maybe it's that he was the only one that didn't try to change how I felt or treat me any different. The only emotion I got from him was that he cared and that he just knew it'd get better. Almost as if he'd seen all this happen before and he knew I could do it. Maybe it's just the fact that he's the one who was sent to watch over me, I don't know.

I'll take whatever it is that has me feeling like I can fight this monster. I can't let Beast kill this bastard, it's my job. He wants me to have the chance or he'd have splattered his brains all over the back wall already. I'm not an idiot when it comes to how these guys work.

"James. I should've fucking cut your head off when I had the chance." He called him James. He knows him. Of course they know him. He has a personal vendetta against them all and I became the target the second I came into the house.

"Now you wouldn't wanna do that and spoil all the fun, would you?"

"Give me one good reason why I shouldn't. I'm more than sure the only reason I haven't already blown your brains out is because I have a feeling Blade and Switch want to personally end you. I bet they have a special dance for you to do before you take your last breath."

"Is this the way you're going to talk to your future club President?"

"That'll never fucking happen." Beast's voice is more of a roar as he responds.

"It's my club by blood. Blade doesn't deserve to sit at the head of my table and act like he was a son to my father." James releases my hair and I fall against the cabinet behind me. My head is throbbing even more now, but I make myself concentrate on what they're saying.

"If Blade didn't deserve it, I wouldn't be standing next to him every fucking day. You think blood makes you a leader? It takes fucking balls to run a club and we all know that's something you've never had." James moves further away so I take the opportunity to grab a knife from the block and lunge straight for him. Beast doesn't hesitate before he shoots twice. He nails him in both of his knees and James drops to the ground. The shots echo in the house and scare me more than I thought they would and I jump back against the wall and hold my chest.

"Why did you shoot him? I had him."

"You still do. I'm just going to make sure you have every chance to give this fucker what he deserves. How is your head?" He nods upwards and for another second I get to see the caring side of Beast.

"You know if you keep worrying about me, I'm going to think you're some kind of softie."

"Go get my phone and call Blade." I look at James on the ground screaming between us and don't leave the room until I watch Beast grip James' jacket and start to drag him out the door. "Hurry up. I'm going to need your help out here."

My heart is racing fast as I move through the house trying to find his phone. I open the door to the room that was closed before and see it on the bed. There are screens on one wall that show different views of the entire house and the land surrounding us. He's been here the entire time and he just let James come in and get to me before he stopped him. I'm not even sure what to think about that, but it makes me feel better knowing he could at least see me most of the time.

Glancing quickly, I don't see a screen showing the bathroom I was in, but who knows if it was also in view when I was taking my shower. I only take the time to scan over it once before running out of the room to help Beast. I have no idea what I'm in for, but I know I need to see this through so I can have some closure on everything that happened to me.

When I open the front door I can hear James crying out in pain coming from the right side of the house. It takes me a minute to process what I'm seeing when I turn the corner, but I quickly see where this is headed.

"You made a big fucking mistake coming for one of ours. When you attack one of us, we consider it a direct hit to us all."

"You can torture me all you want. But she will always feel me deep inside her. I'll fucking live on in that bitch's nightmares and when I do, she'll hear my laughter as I tear up her ass over and over again." His words repulse me and for a slight moment I consider going back inside and letting Beast deal with this on his own. Seeing James sprawled out proves Beast is more than capable of doing it by himself.

"Oh mother fucker, I'm going to enjoy this more than you can ever imagine. She won't dream of you, but if she does she'll have brand new memories to keep her warm at night." Beast tightens the last knot on the rope and sends James spinning when he lifts him off of his feet. He's tied by his arms to a two by four piece of wood against his back. Beast lights up a cigarette before he begins to walk toward me.

"Did your brother answer?" Shit, I haven't dialed his number yet, so I rush to do it as Beast walks past. My eyes lock on James hanging from a tree in front of me as the call tries to connect for what feels like minutes. I find myself walking slowly toward him even though I know I shouldn't. He looks completely different now that the roles are reversed. The fear in his eyes almost makes me feel sorry for him, but a different memory flashes through my head reminding me why he can't get away with what he's done to me. What if he does it to someone else?

I step in front of him just as he stops swaying from side to side. His eyes pierce into mine and for a second I can't look into them. It isn't until I play back more of the torture he put me through that I find the strength to look him in the eyes.

"Everything changes so quickly, doesn't it?" My voice even surprises me as I get enough courage to speak over the lump in my throat that's been suffocating me since I saw him in the house.

"I'll make sure I visit you every night and every time someone is fucking you I'll be there in the back of your head reminding you that I'm the one that controls you. Don't you see? I have nothing to lose hanging here, so torture me all you want. I'm already headed to hell, but at least I won't have to deal with the righteous assholes that stole everything from me."

"Shut the fuck up before I shoot you in the throat too." Beast walks up behind me and this time he doesn't scare me. I'm so deep in thought about everything James is saying that I barely even hear him. "Piper. You're gonna get closure tonight. I'm handing it to you on a fucking silver platter. You need this and just know James will die tonight whether it be by your hand or mine." I hear Beast dropping things on the ground before I look back at him.

Guns, knives, a torch, crowbars, giant clamp looking contraptions, and so many tools I can't even process all of them. "We have all night if that's what it takes. We can take this as slow as you want, or we can end it quick, but you will get your closure and know this fucker is gone forever." This is Beast's fucked up way of making me better and sadly it's perfect for me. I don't know what that says about my character, but this is what I need more than anything. It's what I needed all those years ago and for sure what I need today.

"Take your pick." He points to the ground and I take my time trying to decide. For some reason the blow torch calls to me. It just seems like it would be the most logical thing to start with since I want to torture him some before he goes.

Beast laughs as I pick up the blowtorch. "Shit is about to get real James. I think you may have fucked with the wrong girl." I glance over at Beast and watch him cross his arms and stand with his legs a part like a bouncer would. It seems as though he may find even more pleasure in this than I will, but I'll take it. Him being here is making this possible. I just hope my head can handle what my heart is about to do to this man.

I light up the torch and walk closer to James. He starts to make an obnoxious sound as he laughs from what I would guess is nervousness.

"I want to make sure I know you'll never do this to another woman. Keep laughing, because you won't be laughing when I'm through with you." I get close enough for him to feel the heat of the fire near his face. "Seven. There were seven of you against me. That is the most fucked up part about all of this. I have to find the rest of them and make sure they get the same fate as you, if they haven't already been dealt with by my brother." I choose not to mention Switch. For some reason I still feel like I need to protect him and keep James from knowing I'm connected to him.

I change my mind about starting with the blowtorch as my back burns from the cut that's still fresh enough to make me not forget. Grabbing a switchblade knife and clicking it open before I walk up to him makes me feel even more powerful with a weapon in each hand. These are the only two things I'll need to get the job done, but who knows where I'll take this once I get started.

I let the blade slide over his shirt making sure to cut his skin as I do. His shirt falls open and I make six more cuts as he grits his teeth and yells through each of them. Each cut becomes easier. I find myself watching the blood drip down his skin as I make each slice. It mesmerizes me, so I take my time with each one. I've blocked out everything else in the world and find some clarity as the blood from the last cut comes to surface. Seven. Seven cuts. I wish I could've cut deeper, but he can still feel these as the blood slowly drains from his body. What I realize in this very moment is that I'm not broken. In fact, I may be stronger in this moment than I've been for most of my life.

The roar of the blowtorch pulls me back to reality. I move it slowly toward him before he begins to scream. He knows what I'm about to do. His jeans burn slowly as his cries become unrecognizable. He's not wearing any underwear but his nasty pubic hairs singe instantly as I burn this man's dick.

I don't smell him burning. I don't hear him screaming. I don't hear my own heartbeat. I hear the sound of the torch as it burns him until I've literally watched a dick melt from fire. That is an image that I've burnt into my memory and I hope like hell if he makes it to my thoughts in the future, that is what I see.

I step back and make myself listen to him. I make myself look into his tortured eyes before I turn off the torch and set it back on the ground. I could cut his throat and end him right here. I could watch his blood drip from his lifeless body until I feel complete closure, but honestly I already have what I need to walk away from this and never look back.

"Beast. Thank you." I wrap my arms around his giant body before I pick up my last torture tool. I'm ready for this to be over and there's only one thing that comes to mind. I slide the sharp serrated steel across the front of his throat and find myself watching the blood again. *Is it fucked up that this keeps hypnotizing me?*

James's body starts to convulse while his own blood pools underneath him in the dirt. The sounds of him choking on his own blood gives me a dark satisfaction, more than I thought possible when I plotted my own revenge in my head over the past few days.

My mind finally kicks in and says it's not enough, so I lift the blade over my head, grab onto it with both hands and then stab it into his chest, making sure to hit him right in his stone cold heart. He makes a few gurgling sounds before his head drops and his body becomes motionless.

I just killed a man. No, I just killed a monster.

The sound of a truck driving up should pull me from staring at him, but it doesn't. Beast moves in behind me and wraps his arms around me while I hold the knife down at my side. "Remind me never to fuck with you. You act like your damn brother out here."

Slow and steady footsteps tell me its Blade and I'm guessing Switch. I can't process anything except the fact that I need a shower to remove James from my life completely. His blood still stains my skin and the last thing I want to do is leave it on me longer than necessary.

I step forward and Beast releases his hold on me before I drop the knife to the ground at my feet. Their voices become mumbled as I walk to the house, never looking anyone in the eye as I pass by. I see Switch's boots stop in front of me before I can feel his arms pull me in for a hug like I've never had in my life. "That was the last one. We got the rest of them."

I finally get a deep breath after he speaks to me. It's as if a thousand pounds just left my shoulders and for the first time I feel like there's going to be life after all of this. Switch kisses my lips then holds me for a long time and I feel a single tear, not because I'm sad but because I can finally feel it's over. I push back on Switch, take him by the hand and lead him inside.

"Please just wait for me while I shower. I promise we can talk after, but I need to get this off of me now." I look down at my hands and see bright red blood all over me. He lets me walk away and I love him for that. I need this shower more than anything right now.

Opening the shower door, I step inside and let the water rinse me, clothes and all. Overwhelming hysteria begins to swarm my head and before I have a chance to truly panic, I hear the door open and see Switch's large body moving toward me. He kicks off his boots and then opens the shower door and steps inside with me. The water soaks our clothes instantly, but neither of us focus on that. He wraps his arms around me and pulls me in tight and simply holds me while the pent up tears run down my face.

I missed him so much. How could I ever consider not having him in my life?

Chapter Seventeen

Switch

Fucking Piper, come on! I need you to wake up.

It's been hours and I'm coming unglued just sitting at the side of her bed watching her sleep. I hauled her ass to the doctor as soon as our shower was over. She said she got the all clear from the doctor, but how the fuck would I know? She went in when I dropped her off at the door. She went in without me and they wouldn't let me back in her room. Shit got completely insane for a few minutes until she called me and told me to calm the fuck down. I won't apologize for wanting to be with her when she went through even more evaluations, but I can't trust anyone with her life anymore.

Shit. I need to see her eyes now. I need to hear her voice and know she's alright. I need to know that we're going to be fine and that she's coming home with me as soon as she feels better.

I can't believe what she did to James. I had no idea she had that in her and I feel guilty as fuck for not being here for her when she went through all of that. He never should've gotten to her, yet he did. I can't even blame Beast. He did everything perfectly, even luring James into the house when he knew he was outside. I never would've waited for him to come in and would've probably lost him in this fucking forest when I went out guns blazing into the open.

I look at her brown hair sprawled over her face and fight the urge to brush it out of the way so I can see her. She's still my poison. She makes me insane, but the thought of being without her is so much worse than the chaos I feel when she's near.

"Jesus, Piper. How much longer do I have to wait to hear your voice?" My intended whisper didn't really come out as one and she begins to stir. *Good. I'm fucking impatient and need to talk to her.*

"Hey you." Her voice is raspy as she shifts in the bed so she can see me. She looks like she's lost weight since I last saw her. I can see it in her face now that I'm looking straight into it.

"How do you feel?" I reach out and put my hand on her leg and watch her eyes move to where I'm touching her. She moves immediately so I'm forced to move my hand away. I know better than to fucking rush things after she was attacked like that. What the fuck is wrong with me? I need to respect her space, but that's hard when all I want to do is wrap her the fuck up and never let her go.

"Everything you did back there…" My gut aches with fucking guilt for letting all of this happen to her. I hate this shit and need her to know I'll do everything to never let it happen again. "I will never let anything happen like this again." I feel the anger and frustration still swelling up inside me even further. It silences me because I can't fucking speak over this terrible feeling I have.

"Why are you acting crazy?" She reaches for my hand and pulls it toward her.

"You had me fucking worried, the second we found out we started racing here and…"

"Shhh, get in bed with me. I want to feel you next to me, we can talk later." She moves over to make room for me, but not until she looks at me with those perfect eyes. The whole world melts and everything feels fine; I can't say how, but the look she gives me calms me. I move in next to her even though the hospital bed isn't big enough for my big ass. It gives me a reason to wrap around her and hold her like I've been wanting to do for days.

"I'll always be here for you, Piper." I inhale her hair as I pull her against my chest. She shifts until she's against my chest and then she allows me to hold her. The nurses come in, but never say a word. I can feel that she's still awake, but I let them all believe she's sleeping. This is the best therapy for her. Hell, it's exactly what I need.

"I'm going to miss you taking care of me." My entire body locks up when she speaks. What the fuck does she mean 'miss'?

"You'll never *miss* me. You're gonna be so fucking tired of my ass soon." She shifts out of my arms and begins to get out of bed before I grab her arm to stop her.

"Please don't," she whispers as she drops her head and speaks away from me.

"You fucking don't. Don't pull away from me and you sure as fuck don't stop talking to me." I sit up in the bed to get closer to her.

"I have to."

"No you don't. All I've wanted since this happened was to move back time and fix it all for you, yet somehow you found a way to fix it yourself. I'll never leave you again and I'll always be here to protect you, even if your stubborn ass doesn't want it. And fuck if I ever let you out of my sight again."

"Don't make this harder than it has to be. I can't live like that and I wouldn't think you'd want me to." I don't want her to be in danger, but being away from me will be even worse.

"Fine. I'll leave the club just to make sure you're safe." Her eyes go wide as she comprehends what I'm saying. I stand and walk around the bed to where she is before I lift her hand in mine to bring her to her feet. "I mean every fucking word when I say I'll do anything to make sure you're safe. This shit will never happen to you again for as long as I live."

"Switch, I can't force you to leave the club. It's your life. Those are your brothers and they'd do anything for you."

"And they'll understand why I have to go." I pull her face so that she's looking me straight in the eyes as I say what I need to say. "I'll either spend my entire life looking for you, or you can just embrace the fact that I want to be with you. You can't walk away from what we have, just like I couldn't." Tears fill her eyes and she swallows hard and I think for one short second I have her in the palm of my hands.

"I'm pregnant." My soul freezes. My heart stops and my hands tense up next to her face. She can feel the change in me, no matter how hard I tried to disguise it. I know this means it could be mine. I also know it means it could also be James'. I try to recover quickly, but I know she saw the shock spread across my face before I had the chance to process it all.

"Perfect. This baby needs his father. Now there's no way in hell you're walking away from me." She lays her hand on my arm and pulls it away from her face slowly as she looks me in the eyes. She's telling me no with her expression, but I refuse to listen. Fuck this. She deserves to have a man who would do anything for her and if me saying I'd leave the club for her doesn't prove how much I love her, then nothing will.

"Stop. You know it may not even be yours…"

"No you fucking stop. It is mine. This baby is *mine*. No matter who laid the fucking seed, this baby will always know me as his father." Fucking tears well up in my eyes for the first time in my adult life. How in the fuck I'm ready for this, I'll never know. But the second I saw the hurt in her eyes I knew what I wanted in my life. I want her. All of her. "Piper. You came into my life like a fucking hurricane. I haven't been the same since I met you and I don't want to ever be. You are the strongest woman I've ever met and I can't imagine myself without you. You've consumed my fucking mind since I met you. I'm not going to take no for an answer. I want you. All of you."

"Switch. I can't take you away from your life."

"Then don't try to leave me. Because you are my life." I move in close to her and for the first time in my life I'm resorting to this mushy shit that I always avoid, but for her I'll do anything to get my feelings across. "You. Not the club." I wipe her tears away with my thumbs and when the nurse comes in we never lose eye contact.

"The doctor said you can be released. We're working on the paperwork now." Piper just tells her thank you without ever breaking her focus from me.

"You do realize you're going to get tired of me. I'll drive you crazy." She says it with a smile and I finally feel like I've gotten through to her. For a second I thought I was going to have to chase her across the fucking country until I could convince her that I'm serious.

"Every fucking day." The smile on my face feels nice. It's been a very long time since I've felt like this. I'm sure she was the reason for it even then.

Epilogue

Piper

He feels so good against me. The way Switch has been protecting me has honestly made a little crazy, but I know where he's coming from and appreciate him more than I can even say.

"Beast, you pussy ass. Since when do you not drink?" I'm working the bar in the clubhouse tonight for their weekly meeting. I have Switch against my back and Beast sitting at the end of the bar.

"Since I fuckin' don't feel like it." He doesn't even smile when I give him hell, but I know he loves it. He told me once that he feels like I'm a little sister to him now. Who knew when I moved back here that I'd end up with this many burly guys watching my every move. To say I'm protected is an understatement.

They all know I'm pregnant. The all know it could be Switch's and they all know it could just as easily not be. I told Switch I'd get a paternity test once the baby is born, but he refuses. He says it doesn't matter what the piece of paper says. I have to love him for that, but the truth is I loved him long before that. We've been through so much and I can't imagine my life without him.

I couldn't let him leave the club, but we're working on the compromise that will be best for our family. He's building a house next to Blade and Tori's that should be done in a few months. Blade was happy to have us moving so close and they talked about how much easier it'll be to keep us safe at all times out there.

The level of security equipment these guys now run through every building makes me insane. I'm just not even sure if they can see me showering and pissing, but I guess I don't need to worry about any of that. I'm sure Switch and Blade would take care of my privacy being protected.

Beast leaves the bar and Switch spins me around and lifts me by the ass until I'm wrapped around his waist.

"Fuck, Piper. Who knew you'd look so damn gorgeous with a little belly bump." It's been four months since the attack. Four months since I first fucked Switch and I do have a little belly already. It's strange to look down and see my body changing so fast, but Switch constantly reminds me how sexy I look. He truly can't keep his hands off of me.

It took me a few weeks to really feel connected to him fully again during sex. It wasn't the rape that haunted me, it was the baby. I worried we'd hurt it or that I'd lose it with all the stress my body had been under. Once the doctor assured me that we had a healthy baby and sex was completely fine, it was on. I couldn't get enough of that man. In fact, I'm pretty sure we spent four days never leaving our bed.

"You know you're ready to take me to your old bed. These guys will have to listen to my moaning."

"No fucking way. I'll take you to the house and you can scream as loud as you want." We've been staying in the apartment above the Ink House. It's locked down like no other and he never leaves me there by myself. In fact, he hasn't been on a single run or anything since we moved back. He has one job, and that job is me.

"That sounds perfect. If you think we can make it back before I make you stop." My sex life may have increased in the past few weeks. I feel more alive than I have since I found out I was pregnant and he just keeps encouraging me to do things to him that I've wanted to since I first met him.

It's just easy with him. He starts to walk us both through the clubhouse, telling everyone that we're out of here. "I've got to teach this clubwhore a lesson, guys. I'll be back tomorrow."

"Sam Riley Grayson… I am not your clubwhore." His laughter shakes his chest against mine as he pushes us through the front door.

"What are you then? Would you rather me call you my Old Lady?"

"Fuck no. I'm not old enough for that shit."

"Alright, well when you think of what it is you want me to call you, just let me know." He kisses me against the wall outside before he moves us to his truck. The baby isn't allowed to ride on the bike, so we've been in the truck since we moved back. He's stubborn as hell about all of this.

He opens the driver's door and sets me on the seat, but I use this height to wrap my arms around his neck and go in for a kiss that'll get everything moving real fast. Our kisses are passionate. We may not be the best with words, but I know exactly how he feels in his kiss.

"Scoot over. I need in this fucking truck before I fuck you in the parking lot." It doesn't take long and he's crawling over me in the truck and sliding my shirt up over my tits. "Fuck, I love you like this. Always ready for me."

"Always," I whisper against his cheek as he removes his belt and unbuttons his jeans. He moves to do that same to mine and I shift my hips when he grips between my legs, sending electricity through my body. I wait impatiently for him to make me feel like he always does. He knows my body better than I do and fuck if he doesn't know how to make me insane in record time.

What did I do to deserve a guy like this? I have no idea. I only know he loves me with an intensity that I need in my life. The burn of his love keeps me grounded.

"Here, straddle me. I want to watch you take me." He leans the seat back and I kick off my shorts before I throw my leg over his and position myself. His hands grip my sides and he leans me back until I've got both palms on the windshield and dash behind me. He moves me up and down his erection and I watch his eyes never leave where his dick is sliding in and out of me.

"Fuck you're so goddamn sexy." His grip shifts and he slides me toward him until he's so deep inside me that it takes my breath away. I close my eyes as I take him in all the way. Moving on him is easy; it's like second nature at this point. Getting lost in him is one of my favorite parts of the day.

"Feel me, Piper." He whispers over my lips, so I open my eyes and take in everything he's saying. "Feel everything I'm saying to you. Feel me touch you." He moves his hand up my back until he pulls me closer with his hand on my neck. "Feel me fuck you." *Oh god. I feel you.*

"Feel me love you. Feel me want you more than I want anything else in the world." His thrusts are slow and steady. It's an unusual pace for us, but one that speaks volumes right now. I can feel him, but I could before he even knew what he was feeling. I love this man so much.

"I feel you." Those three words are the last coherent thing I can say because he takes me to an entirely different place with the next drive of his hips.

This is my life. He is my life. We may be insane together, but I could never imagine the madness if we were apart!

This series is only getting started…
Just #WatchUs for the next in the series!

To receive a text on the next release day…
Text "Seven" to 213-802-5257!

BOOKS BY HILARY STORM

Six

Seven

Rebel Walking Series

In A Heartbeat

Heaven Sent

Banded Together

No Strings Attached

Hold Me Closer

Fighting the Odds

Never Say Goodbye

Whiskey Dreams

Bryant Brothers Series

Don't Close Your Eyes

Alphachat.com Series

Pay for Play

Two can Play

Elite Forces Series

ICE

FIRE

STONE

Stalk Hilary Here

Website: www.hilarystormwrites.com

Facebook:

https://www.facebook.com/pages/Hilary-Storm-Author/492152230844841

Goodreads:

https://www.goodreads.com/author/show/7123141.Hilary_Storm?from_search=true

Twitter: @hilary_storm

Instagram: http://instagram.com/hilstorm

Tumblr: https://www.tumblr.com/blog/hilarystorm

Snapchat: hilary_storm

Spotify: Hilary Storm

Stalk Dylan Here

Facebook: @DylanHorsch

Instagram: @DylanHorsch

Snapchat: Dylan_Horsch

Twitter: @DylanHorsch

Acknowledgements

By Hilary

Nathan… you make this all possible for me. If I didn't have you, I'd never be able to do half the stuff I do! Thank you for always supporting me no matter what my crazy mind comes up with! My kiddos… you sacrifice so much for your mom to follow her dreams. I can see the proud look on your faces when you talk about what I do and I can only hope I've taught you that you are your only limits in life!

Dylan… Holy hell we did it. It seems I remember you saying you can't write… but you have lots of material. Well… I'm calling bullshit my friend. You were amazing to write with and I love how involved you are with the characters. It truly feels like you helped create them all even though we didn't even know each other when I wrote Six. I guess in a weird way you did help create them. You are just beginning your career in all of this and I can't be more proud that you've trusted me to be your partner in all of this. It's been an amazing adventure and the best part of it is we've only just begun! I can't wait to see where we go from here! #WatchUS

Dana… How could I ever live without you? I couldn't. You make my work so damn gorgeous! Thank you for always getting my stuff done quickly and keeping my graphics top of the line in the industry. You're incredible!

Kellie… thank you for cleaning up our messes! You are a great friend and I love that I get to keep it in my circle with you as an editor for my books!

Nick and Golden… Thank you for making a great cover for this book! It's a perfect reflection of Switch and I knew I had to have it!

Amanda and Lindsey… you two keep me grounded daily. Thank you for always checking on me and giving me the real advice I need always!

Hall… Thank you for being you. Not for anything you do… just being fucking real and a solid in this industry.

To my readers… THANK YOU. Without your support at signings and on social media, I'd forget why I do what I do. You make this so much fun for me and I'm proud as hell that I have the best readers out there!

Acknowledgements

By Dylan

Mom, there isn't enough words to say thank you for inspiring me to be the best that I can be and giving me the courage to chase my dreams even when the world wanted to write me off and tell me I wasn't shit. It's because of you that all things are possible for me.

Hilary, where would I be without you. For buying my first cover and giving me the opportunities I've had in the industry I could never thank you enough. You inspired me to write and look at this crazy adventure we've set fourth because of it. We have so much ahead and I can't wait!

To my family and friends that support me day in and day out, I promise you the best is still yet to come. I've only gotten started on all I have to accomplish and I can't wait for you all to see what's ahead for me.

And to everyone who has followed me on this journey, it's because of you that this is possible. Without your support, the shares, the likes, supporting my work, I wouldn't be here without you. Thank you so much everyone and know that there isn't enough thank you'd in the world or enough pages to thank every single one of you for the joy you've brought me in my life. Now hopefully I can bring a little to yours!

Made in United States
Orlando, FL
15 August 2022

21046410R00104